JAN JONES
THE UNPLEASANTNESS AT THE BELLADONNA CLUB

FENCROSS PARVA
BOOK 2

The Unpleasantness at the Belladonna Club
copyright © 2023 by Jan Jones

Kindle Edition

Jan Jones has asserted her right to be identified as the author of this Work in accordance with the Copyright, Designs and Patents Act 1988.

All rights reserved. No part of this publication may be reproduced, distributed, or transmitted in any form or by any means, including photocopying, recording, or other electronic or mechanical methods, without the prior written permission of the copyright holder, except in the case of brief quotations embodied in critical reviews and certain other non commercial uses permitted by copyright law. For permission requests, email the author at the address below.

This is a work of fiction. All names, characters and places spring entirely from the author's own imagination. Any resemblance to actual persons, living or dead, is coincidental.

Cover design and formatting www.jdsmith-design.com

All enquiries to jan@jan-jones.co.uk

JAN JONES
THE UNPLEASANTNESS AT THE BELLADONNA CLUB

FENCROSS PARVA
BOOK 2

Welcome to Fencross Parva
Life, love and the occasional dead body

DEDICATION

For village club organisers everywhere

It would be a far poorer world without you

DRAMATIS PERSONAE

In Fencross Parva

Annie Dearlove ~ artist, reluctant Airbnb provider (Hope Cottage)

Kenelm Gray ~ police inspector (Hope Cottage)

Calli Nelson ~ librarian (Doctor's Corner)

Gideon Frost ~ carpenter (The Lodge)

Violet Renshaw ~ president of gardening club (Riverdene bungalow)

Minna Saxon ~ doormat (Mulberry Lane)

Dinah & Jolyon Gray ~ Kenelm's parents (Fencross Manor)

Lady Honoria Gray ~ dowager (Fencross Manor)

Topsy Candour - nonagenarian (Lavender House)

Suzy Emmet ~ Topsy's carer (Lavender House)

Bessie ~ proprietor of the *Cosy Kettle* café (Mulberry Lane)

Rev Robin Taylor-Bigelow ~ vicar of St Athelm (Rectory)

Bunty Taylor-Bigelow ~ garden designer (Rectory)

Phyllis Winterbottom ~ WI chair

Julie Bamber ~ WI secretary

Pat Williams ~ dog lover

Bonita Ellwood ~ gossip

Jerry Ellwood ~ estate agent (New Parade)

The Police

Constable Dee Bryce ~ PC with attitude

Detective Superintendent 'Speedy' Macready ~ it's in the name

Elsewhere

Heather Meadows ~ wild foraging expert

Sarah Gray ~ Kenelm's ex-wife

Eithan Bryce ~ Dee's husband, car mechanic

CHAPTER ONE

Annie Dearlove was thirteen months into renting out her spare rooms with Airbnb and hated it with every fibre of her being. She glared at the latest yuppie couple standing obstructively in the kitchen between her and her studio, and wished for the thousandth time that an artist's income was as reliable and regular as the tax assessors whimsically imagined it to be.

"The description on the website states this is a three hundred year old cottage with no mod cons," she said between gritted teeth. "There are videos of the bedrooms. What made you think a television and coffee machine would have materialised since you booked two days ago?"

The young man's mouth was set in a petulant line. "I don't care for your attitude."

Nor I yours, sunshine. Did nobody ever teach you manners?
"I'm telling it like it is. The reviews for Hope Cottage make frequent mention of my no-nonsense approach."

"We assumed they were joking. Anyone would."

"I want to see the room the murdered architect stayed in," complained the young woman, pouting.

Oh, please let the wind change and you stay that way.
"Impossible. That room is booked for the next six months. Was there anything else?"

"WiFi code."

"Upstairs in your room along with the pub opening times, restaurant booking details, takeaway phone numbers, village map and instructions on how *not* to let the dogs and hens out. If that's all, I'm busy. Enjoy your stay."

"Library," said the woman sullenly. "How do we get to the library where he was murdered?"

Annie had given up correcting people. "The library is marked on the map. Walk along to the High Street, turn left and it's just before the church." She waited a beat and then added, "It closed an hour ago."

The pair retreated upstairs in disgust.

"What I don't understand," remarked Kenelm Gray, who'd been sitting at the old oak table scrolling through his phone messages throughout this altercation, "is how you have any bookings at all."

Annie narrowed her eyes at the tenant of the disputed bedroom. Even steady rent, ash-blond hair and a chiselled resemblance to David Bowie didn't give him the right to criticise. "If you're not careful, I'll tell them you were the arresting officer."

"That's harsh."

"It's true."

"Seriously, I'm impressed at how you've made a feature out of being phenomenally rude to your visitors. I know I'm angry with the world at the moment, but why are you?"

She growled in frustration. She'd known Kenelm forever in the way children in a village always did know each other, no matter what their station in life. It was disorienting that after some forty years of disparaging him as a product of the class system, she was reluctantly having to change her mind.

"It's like this," she said. "My Aunty Dora, who you won't remember because she was older than Mum, was once a free spirit who ran away to drama college."

"Good God. From Fencross Parva?"

"Don't be so feudal. It was the 1970s. Ordinary people did that sort of thing in those days. Just because your lot up at the Manor are still stuck in the Edwardian era, it doesn't mean the rest of us have to be."

Kenelm winced. "Point taken."

"Aunty Dora was a good actress, but she lived entirely in the present and never gave a thought to the future. When the work and the men dried up, she had a mortgage and no savings. She had to do something to make ends meet, so she took in paying guests. She hated having them in her house, was disastrously anxious to please and they walked all over her. Like her, I need the money. Like her, I hate having strangers in my home. Unlike her, I prefer rage to misery. Most visitors are fine with a hands-off approach. I'm only actively rude to the people who deserve it."

That wasn't the whole story, but it was more than she told most people and it was exasperating she'd let out so much. It must be Kenelm's neutral, professional air leading her on. If he was likely to stay as a long-term lodger, she'd have to watch that. The microwave pinged. He got up to release his dinner. Annie quickly crossed to her studio door before he had a chance to resume the conversation.

She loved her studio. Just thinking about it eased her tension. She'd converted it from the long stone outhouse as soon as Grandma had died, joyfully scrubbing the begrimed windows to flood the room with light, using the old scullery sink for her clean-up area and throwing out decades of mangles, wash tubs and animal troughs to create a cool, uncluttered space. It held her hopes and dreams and right now she wanted to wrap the calm, whitewashed walls around her and breathe its peace. She was halfway inside when the back door opened.

"Annie, are you horribly busy?" asked Calli Nelson in a despairing tone. "Hi, Kenelm. Sorry, I didn't mean to interrupt."

"You aren't," said Annie. "I *was* just about to do some work. What's the matter, found another body?"

Calli paled. "Don't even joke about that. It's this WI meeting tonight. Lady Honoria practically ordered me to join, but I really don't fancy it on my own. Gideon told me you always went so…"

Annie's vision of an evening of painting vanished in a puff of consternation. How could it be WI night already? Where had the month gone? Lost in a blur of laundry and hens and dogs and invasive strangers and not enough solid creativity. Dear God, this wasn't living.

"Damn, I'd forgotten. Yes, okay, I'll give you a knock on my way past."

Kenelm looked around in surprise. "Really? I would never have pegged you for a Women's Institute person."

She twitched one shoulder as if her explanation didn't matter. "I can do socialising when I have to. I used to take Mum to the meetings before she stopped recognising anyone. Now I have a monthly sale table there to go towards her care home fees. People remember me guiltily when they need to buy cards and paintings as presents. Ten percent goes to WI funds." Before either of them thought about looking sympathetic, she said, "Why are you cluttering up the kitchen, anyway? When I agreed to you lodging, you told me you were always working."

"I've got the evening off and so far my chief hasn't recalled me. It's very unsettling. Would you like me to walk the dogs if you're going out? I can arrest someone for loitering to keep my hand in."

Annie had an ignoble struggle with herself and lost. "If you mean it, yes please. Just rub Sofi down if she jumps in the brook again. Who's the speaker, Calli, any idea?"

"I don't know, but the talk is on foraging. Lady H thought it was likely to be slides of wild mushrooms on paper doilies."

Annie's heart sank. "Oh no, please don't let it be someone Violet Renshaw has found. At least it won't be Violet herself, the committee have got too much sense for that."

Calli's brow creased. "Who? I don't know her. She isn't a library member."

"Lucky you. I wish I could say the same. One of my least favourite people, and that's saying something. She's the president of the belladonna club."

"The *what*?" said Kenelm, pausing in the act of transferring his meal to a plate.

"The Fencross Parva Gardening Club. Hasn't your mother told you about it?"

"Probably. That's not to say I remember."

She grinned at his dry tone. "Belladonna is the Latin name for deadly nightshade."

"I know that, but I still don't understand," said Calli.

Annie leant against the doorframe. "You will when you hear the whole story. Dinah Gray re-christened it a few years ago, soon after Violet muscled on to the committee. The gardening club had done the church flowers that week, and the choirboys were sitting underneath this artistic arching arrangement of black and red berries..."

Calli gasped and put her hand to her mouth. "No."

"True. Apparently they were reaching up stealthily during the sermon and stripping the berries off to ping across the chancel. Then one of them made the mistake of popping a couple between his far-from-angelic lips."

"Ah," said Kenelm, enlightened. "Yes, I do remember now. Fortunately for those boys, my mama can recognise white bryony and deadly nightshade at fifty paces. First and only time she's ever interrupted the vicar in the middle of a service. I almost wish I'd been there to see it."

Annie laughed. "Me too. Mum said Dinah marched up to the pulpit, stopped Rev Silver in mid-sentence and ordered the whole rear pew outside to find Dr Gotobed. He was furious at being hauled away from his Sunday pint to dish out emetics. Didn't mince his words when he found out why."

"Good for Uncle Matthew," said Calli with a chuckle.

"So, it's been called the belladonna club ever since, much to their annoyance. Violet is pure poison. Convinced she knows everything, even when she doesn't. I've had several run-ins with her regarding Fencross Common. She's one of those saccharine women who always gets the best seat by looking sorrowfully at whoever was about to sit in it, ditto the largest piece of cake and the fullest cup of tea. After the belladonna incident she went around saying it was the parents' fault for not bringing their children up properly and that they should be grateful to her for introducing them to a valuable life-lesson."

"She sounds ghastly," said Calli, turning to go. "I'm glad she isn't a library member. She'd probably instruct me on how to shelve my own books. See you later. Thanks again."

CHAPTER TWO

Another month, another meeting, thought Annie with an oppressive sense of *deja vu* as she trundled her case of stock through the church hall door that Calli was holding open. The familiar warring scents of mothball, menthol and mixed floral top notes met her. She saw Calli wrinkle her nose and wondered if suggesting they come to the meeting together was a cunning plan by Gideon Frost to forge a friendship between them. He might be her oldest ally, but he did have a tiresome habit of trying to heal the world. On the other hand, at least he was still here and largely unchanged. When you've lived in the same village for your whole forty-three years, most of your original mates have either shafted you, turned boring or moved away.

Calli was a relatively unknown quantity. A widow of around Annie's age, she'd moved to Fencross Parva to look after her uncle Dr Gotobed last year. That was just after Mum had got so much worse and had to go into the care home. The guilt about that decision, the utter relief once it had been effected and the worry about how to continue to pay for it had been overwhelming. Annie had been pretty much at breaking point for months. Forging new friendships was the last thing on her mind, even if she'd been the sociable sort, which she wasn't.

Aunty Dora's modest legacy - and thank goodness the sale of Dora's house had gone through before the economy tanked - had taken the financial heat off Annie to a certain extent, but by then Dr Gotobed had died and Calli had been grieving and turning his former surgery into a village subscription library by way of therapy. Now that Calli and Gideon were an item it was time to make a proper effort getting to know her. She hoped she remembered how.

"Cheers," she said. "Why they don't ever hook at least one of these doors open I'll never know." *Habit. Tradition. No one ever has, so no one ever will. It was partly why you left, remember? And look how well that worked out.*

"Maybe one of the committee is a fan of 1940s speakeasy movies," joked Calli.

Annie was surprised into a laugh. "Where you give a secret knock, speak 'friend' and enter? Oh, I wish. I can just see Lady H and Dinah Gray shutting all the men out, opening a beer with their teeth and settling down to watch James Cagney, can't you?"

Calli's face was a picture at the thought of the Fencross Manor ladies doing any such thing. "Um, no."

"Beautiful image though. Talk of the devil, here they come. Nab us a couple of chairs on the back row while I set out my table. I always put it here so people have to go past me to get to the loo."

"Good thinking. Remind me to bring a tube of extra strong mints next month. Nothing better for staving off competing aromas. First thing they teach you at library school."

"It is a bit much, isn't it? Decades of WI meetings, jumble sales, scouts, Brownies, village clubs and church suppers. And no one ever opens the windows."

She nodded a greeting to Dinah, glad Kenelm's decision to board at Hope Cottage after the break-up of his marriage, rather than moving back to Fencross Manor, hadn't produced a coolness with his mother. She covered the ancient trestle table with a drape and did a head count. All the usual suspects were present. Lady Honoria and Dinah were at the front, the better for Lady H to fix the speaker with a gimlet eye and cough pointedly if she went over her allotted time. Suzy Emmet was settling old Topsy Candour into the chair next to Lady H and reminding her, after a look at the long table where books, pamphlets and an array of very smart food containers were laid out, that she'd be back at nine o'clock to walk her home.

Calli was also eyeing the front of the hall. "This all looks worryingly formal. I'm telling myself socialising will be good trade for the library. If people see me around the village more often, they might be tempted to join."

"It works for me," replied Annie. "Much as I'd prefer to be in the studio, the more I'm seen, the more it reminds people to buy greetings cards from me rather than from shops. Talking of which, can you give this to Rhona Lee for the raffle? I always contribute something."

Calli took the hand-painted card. "That's pretty. What is it?"

"Henbane," replied Annie. And at Calli's lifted eyebrows, "What? It's artistic. Good for toothache. Absolutely not a comment on the present company."

Calli chuckled and delivered the card.

"Thanks," said Annie when she returned. "You'll get a name check during the business waffle as a new guest, so be prepared to smile."

"Will do. Who is the very busy powder puff at the front?"

Annie grimaced. "Violet Renshaw. I'm guessing the bony, eager one she's fussing over is the speaker. Yes, look, Phyllis Winterbottom is gliding across in full chairperson mode to welcome her." She turned back to mount a couple of paintings on miniature easels. She had no expectation of selling much, but as one of her former art tutors with more financial acumen than the rest of the faculty put together always said, the more you display, the more professional you look. No one buys stuff they don't see.

"Gosh," remarked Calli, still watching the hall. "Must be the first time I've ever witnessed a scrimmage for the front row of a talk."

Anne gave a snort of laughter. "That'll be the gardening mafia, being foiled by Lady H and Dinah Gray. They'll have to make do with the second and third rows instead."

"They aren't exactly exchanging loving glances with them," said Calli. "Oh, poor Minna Saxon has been squeezed out of her front-row seat by the powder puff."

"Doesn't surprise me. Minna is a walking doormat. As for the less-than-loving glances, that's due to the ongoing church flowers feud. There may be in-fighting galore between themselves, but they always close ranks on outsiders."

"Church flowers?"

"The belladonna club think they should do St Athelm's arrangements all the time. Everyone else knows the Manor has been responsible for the rose window and the Lady Chapel since time immemorial, the school does Palm Sunday and the WI always decorate the church for Advent."

"So they do. I'd forgotten. One time when I was staying here, Aunty Irene was in a huge tizz because she'd promised her bronze dahlias to the WI for the display, but a goat from the Home Farm had got in and eaten the lot. We had to make an emergency dash to three different supermarkets to buy replacements."

"I can't decide whether I want to hear more about the church flowers feud or less," said a new voice.

Annie turned to see a tall, slender woman with rainbow hair, an eyebrow piercing, a row of studs marching up her ear and a beautiful twisting vine tattoo on her arm. There was only one person it could be.

"Hi, Rev Robin," said Calli, confirming her deduction. "I don't know anything about the feud, I'm afraid. You'll need to ask Annie. Have you two met?"

Annie stuck out the hand that wasn't wedging a fragment of card under the leg of a wobbly easel. "Annie Dearlove. Hope Cottage in Mulberry Lane."

"That's the Airbnb, isn't it? Excellent," said Fencross Parva's new vicar with a pleased nod. "Bunty told me to find some local guest houses so we don't need to have anyone to actually stay at the rectory." She looked at Annie's paintings. "Oh my fur and whiskers, these are beautiful. May I buy the one of the wild-flower grave in the cemetery with St Athelm all misty and sun-streaked in the background?"

Annie experienced a profound shock. She supposed the spouse of a well-known garden designer would have to have some sort of artistic appreciation, but even so... "Are you sure? You don't have to. It's the most expensive. I only bring the big ones so the others seem a bargain in comparison."

"Don't be ridiculous, woman, it's stunning. I want it for the wall of my study. I can do you a bank transfer when I get back."

"Sold," said Annie, and put a red sticker on the frame. There was only so much saving others from themselves a person with care home fees to pay could reasonably manage. "I'll bring it over to the rectory tomorrow. I'll even hang it for you."

"Awesome," said Rev Robin. She turned and surveyed the room. "One more favour. May I sit with you?"

This, thought Annie, was turning into an unexpectedly good evening. First Calli proving to have a sense of humour quite as irreverent as Annie's own, and now the new vicar buying her best painting and promising - assuming she'd understood right - to put some Airbnb custom her way. It was almost worth missing an evening's painting. She took her seat in far better heart than usual. Just the meeting itself to get through.

To her surprise, the speaker was very well-informed, unlike the appalling talk on foraging given several years ago to the gardening club by Violet Renshaw herself. That had contained so many errors over the legality of digging up wild plants and putting them in your own garden and gathering hedgerow berries on nature reserves that Annie had got into a furious row with Violet about countryside law right in the middle of the meeting. She and Mum had never gone to a gardening club function again.

After apologising for not being able to stay for the whole evening due to an early start tomorrow on a bookshop tour, the speaker - who rejoiced in the name of Heather Meadows - touched accurately on that very subject, flicked through a selection of commonly confused plants, and then moved smoothly to *Tasty Dishes from Found Ingredients.*

"Does she mean 'found' like when my friend Meriel finds a nice little Sauv Blanc in the mark-down bin at the offie?" murmured Calli.

The muffled explosion of laughter from their row caused the gardening club collective to turn and frown.

"Wild mushroom medley," announced Heather, clicking on a slide of various fungi arranged on a lace doily and breaking open the first air-tight container. The room eyed it with perceptible alarm.

"And just where," enquired Dinah Gray in her clear, well-modulated voice, "do you find wild mushrooms at this time of year?"

"Exotic ingredients aisle at Sainsbury," said Rev Robin, sotto voce.

Annie choked, but Heather was beaming with approval. "A countrywoman. How splendid. You are entirely right. I gathered these myself during the autumn and froze the dish. Would you like to try some? I assure you I have given this talk to many groups and no one has yet been rushed to hospital."

Amidst the slightly forced laughter, Dinah made a resigned face and put the smallest spoonful possible on a finger of bread. "Very nice," she said politely.

You had to hand it to the ladies from the Manor, thought Annie. They always did their duty.

Heather Meadows snapped lid after lid off her colourful containers, explaining the recipes as she went along, then set all the square tubs out on the table beside a pile of paper plates with a genial invitation for people to help themselves. As she moved off, she edged the display of books for sale into slightly more prominence.

Rev Robin sighed. "I suppose I'd better do the pretty," she said, and strolled towards the front.

"Huh. I was promised tea and cake," said Calli.

Annie grinned. "That comes after the WI business and the competition. It's a reward for sticking it out to the end."

A couple of ladies came up to ask Annie how her mother was, drawing out the buying of a gift card until all danger of anyone noticing they hadn't tried the speaker's dishes had passed.

"She has good days and bad days. I'll tell her you asked after her," said Annie. Her face ached with the strain of smiling. You'd think she'd have got over the rage at Mum's dementia by now. Why was it always worse here? *Because her friends are here, the people she grew up alongside. The people she knew and laughed with and played tennis against. And she isn't.*

"Gideon told me," said Calli, giving her hand a squeeze. "I didn't realise before. I'm so sorry."

The practical sympathy was almost harder to bear than the rest. Annie was saved from replying by a warm voice greeting her and a beautifully manicured hand appearing in the corner of her vision to leaf through the cards.

"Now these are marvellous. I've had my eye on them since you began setting up. I love how you've captured the ethereal quality of the plants whilst still leaving them instantly identifiable. Do you do book illustrations at all?"

Annie looked up, startled, to meet the twinkling gaze of Heather Meadows. "I take commissions, if that's what you mean." *Dear God, do I. As many and as often as I can get them.*

"That's splendid. What I have in mind is..."

They were interrupted by a blast of perfume and the cloying, sugary tones of Violet Renshaw. She cavalierly pushed aside Annie's display to make space for a paper plate piled with salad. "You mustn't forget to have some of your own creations, Heather," she said.

"Thank you, dear," said Heather. "That's very thoughtful." When Violet had tottered off, she moved the plate to the far end of the table and restored the paintings to their places. "Occupational hazard. Sorry. Now, for my next book I want to show the plants in the wild in the sort of habitat where people might find them. Sadly, my photography is woeful. Would you be up for sketching small botanical groups like you've done with these larger cards? I'd need a lot, I can email you the list. We could arrange it as a fee or royalties. As your chair naughtily mentioned, there's a teeny regular slot on a countryside television programme in the offing, which should push up sales. I can put my agent in touch with yours, if you like?"

Annie shut her mouth with a snap, then opened it again to answer. "I... yes."

"Good. May I take a business card? Here are my details. I'll be in contact when I get back from my little book tour.

So ridiculous, isn't it? A book tour for stuff you can get for free." Her warm voice and comical smile invited them to join in with her amusement. "Meanwhile, I'd like this lovely thing, please." She put a twenty pound note into Annie's hand and moved off to the front of the hall with a medium-sized montage of wild flowers tucked under her arm.

"Crikey," said Calli into the silence. "I'd better buy one of her books so you know what they're like. I can put in into the library stock." She picked up her purse and followed Heather.

Annie was still in shock when Pat Williams bustled over with one of the square containers. "Is this finished with?" she asked, picking up the untouched plate of salad to tip it in. "Phyllis is panicking about clearing up for the rest of the meeting."

"What? Oh, yes, I..."

But Pat had rushed off to swoop on someone else's selection, dropping the now empty plate into the paper-recycling bin as she went.

"Not bad at all," whispered Calli, sliding back into the chair beside her. "The pamphlets by Violet Renshaw are home-produced and appalling, but Heather Meadows is with a proper reputable publisher, hence the book tour. Here you are. Nice readable text. I'll look her up when I get back. See what else she's done."

"Thanks," said Annie. "You'd better come to everything with me now. You're clearly a lucky charm."

"You'll have trouble fitting me on a bracelet," replied Calli.

Violet gave them a sharp look as she minced past to use the toilets. Evidently she didn't think helpless laughter was at all appropriate after a quality talk. Annie couldn't have cared less. She didn't even mind the smirk on the wretched woman's face when she glanced at all the unsold paintings on her return through the hall. Mind you, that was before Violet's announcement at the end of the meeting.

CHAPTER THREE

Kenelm Gray stood outside the pub, putting his phone away. The familiar outline of his cousin emerged from the lit doorway and passed him the remains of his beer.

"Cheers," said Kenelm.

Gideon Frost made a don't-mention-it gesture. "I'm off to the church hall and thought you might appreciate the rest of your pint out here rather than going back inside for it."

"You'd be right. Christ, Gideon, I had assumed when Sarah decided she wanted space to be herself, the rows would stop."

"And yet."

"And yet." He drained the glass and lined it up on a table with other empties. "I don't even know what she wanted tonight. I don't think she knows herself. I've moved out as she asked. I'm still paying all the bills. I'm texting the boys like a dutiful father. Is it too much to finally have some peace?"

Gideon moved off. "Maybe she expected you to fight."

"We've been fighting for a year. I can't do it any more. I can be the hard man at work. I've lost the stomach for it at home. Where are we going?"

"Well, *I'm* going to the church hall to walk back with Calli. I did say."

"Sweet. Anyone would think you've regressed thirty years. I'll leave you to it. If I'm outside when my mother sallies forth, I'll not only be stuck with escorting her and Lady H home, I'll be invited into the Manor for a nightcap and meaningful interrogation."

Suzy Emmet came flying past. "Are they out yet? I promised Mrs Candour I'd be back for her. Sorry, Inspector Gray, I didn't recognise you without your uniform. Is everything all right?"

"The Women's Institute appears entirely free of trouble," he replied gravely.

Suzy gave an uncertain smile and hurried into the hall.

"Better get a move on," warned Gideon. "People are starting to leave. That's my girl, first one through the door." He lifted an arm to wave at Calli.

Kenelm felt a sharp pang of envy at the delight on Calli's face. It was a long time since Sarah had looked at him like that. Failure gnawed at him. Failure and loneliness.

Calli turned to the person behind her. "Annie, Kenelm's here with Gideon if you want a hand trundling your case."

"I can manage," said Annie, "but if you're after camouflage from Lady H, feel free to trundle. Quickly, though. She's saying gracious goodbyes and trying to stop your mama smacking Violet Renshaw around the head with her own pamphlets. Not that I can blame her for that."

Kenelm's jaw dropped. "Mother is? Really? Why?"

"Come back for a coffee and we'll tell you," said Calli. "Tonight's been a revelation. I had no idea the WI was such an emotional battlefield."

"This I've got to hear," said Gideon. He grinned at Kenelm. "Coming?"

From the hall, he heard his mother's voice, clear and cross. "Yes all right, Honoria. I wanted a word with Annie, but she seems to have left."

"Let's go," said Kenelm hastily.

"It was all perfectly normal until Phyllis Winterbottom asked if there was any other business," said Calli once they were settled in her library with mugs of coffee and a tin of biscuits. "This is not a question I have ever previously associated with incipient violence."

Kenelm sipped the coffee and felt himself relax. He wasn't sure whether it was the company, the ambience of the room or a combination of both. During the day Calli opened her library to the village, but in the evenings it showed itself for what it was: a restful, comfortable sanctuary with deep chairs, velvet curtains and more than the average number of books.

"Go on," said Gideon, chuckling.

"Fortunately the speaker had gone by then. She was really good, by the way, and wants Annie to illustrate her next book. Isn't that fantastic?"

"That's terrific, Annie," said Gideon. "Well done."

Annie looked embarrassed. "It might not come to anything."

"My mother?" Kenelm reminded them.

Calli's look of rebuke told him just how far he'd travelled in being accepted as part of their group. "Kenelm, she'd pay real money, it's important."

"Sorry. Well done, Annie. That's really good news."

Calli gave an approving nod. "So, Annie and I were leafing through Heather Meadows's book waiting for the tea and cake I'd been promised, when Violet Renshaw gets coyly to her feet saying she might have an exciting announcement next month, but right now it's a big secret, it'll put Fencross Parva on the map and she can't say any more until she has confirmation."

Annie spoke. "Everyone is used to Violet. Phyllis replied crisply that if it was a WI matter then she, as chair, ought to be told well before next month. Upon which

Violet looked even more smug and said it was nothing *directly* to do with the WI, but it might affect arrangements for the annual fete."

"The fete?" Kenelm was completely lost now.

Annie nodded. "It's held on the common, if you remember. As soon as Violet said that, your mother knew exactly what she was talking about - as did I - and she leapt up asking how dare Violet even *think* of making a general announcement and if she didn't desist immediately, Dinah was going to frog-march her straight outside for a frank discussion."

Kenelm wondered briefly if some mind-altering drug had been added to the coffee. "We're still talking about my mother, yes? Possibly the most law-abiding woman on the planet?"

"It was nothing to what I was going to do to Violet," said Annie.

"But why?"

"She won't tell me," complained Calli. "She and your mother both shot over to Violet and started hissing away about a marsh. Upon which Phyllis hurriedly closed the meeting, reminded Dinah she was on the refreshment rota and everyone bustled around with tea and cake, seething with either fury, righteous indignation or curiosity. I was hoping you might come over official and force Annie to fill us in."

"Police powers don't work quite like that in this country."

"I can make a good guess," said Gideon. "If it's got Annie fired up, it'll have something to do with the common. If it's roused your mother, Kenelm, then it has to do with plants. Is it, perhaps, an unusual plant you've discovered on the common that Violet has somehow got wind of?"

Annie pushed her untidy dark fringe out of the way

and glowered at him. "Too clever by half, that's your trouble. Yes, okay, there is a rare form of early marsh orchid in one of my squares-of-care that is just starting to come into flower. Dinah is the second guardian because I needed someone with clout and an idea of what it meant. We registered it a couple of years ago and have kept very, very quiet about it. I've had to forcibly stop Violet digging up plants before. If she's researched this one and has decided to announce it to the world in a pathetic bid for five minutes of fame, it could attract unscrupulous plant-hunters."

Kenelm opened his mouth to ask if that was all, but just in time recognised Annie's undercurrent of anger as similar to the emotions simmering around his ex-wife these days. He changed it to a diplomatic, "What can you do?"

"Not a lot," said Annie. "Warn the rare plant people and keep watch. I'd better nip along there now to check on it."

"Violet isn't going to dig it up in the dark," said Calli.

"I don't see her digging it up at all," pointed out Gideon. "She'd lose all credibility at having discovered a rare species if it turned out to be in her own garden. Plus, there wouldn't need to be any special arrangements regarding protecting it during the WI fete, so there would have been no sense in mentioning it." He frowned. "In fact, there wouldn't be anyway. Aren't all your squares-of-care fenced off and festooned with scientific survey labels?"

"Yes, but..."

"It might not be the one you have registered," said Kenelm. "If you've found one instance of it on the common, mightn't the plant also be at a number of different sites?"

"It's possible," conceded Annie, "but if you'd seen the way she looked at me, all sly and victorious, you wouldn't have a doubt either. And then she started on about photographers and regional telly and a double-page spread in some nature magazine that she was going to book. Like I said, she wants her moment of glory."

"There's still no point checking on it now. You'll draw attention to yourself, going out there flashing a torch around. There could be any number of unsavoury characters on the common who might come over to have a look and trample everything."

"Only a policeman could mention unsavoury characters and Fencross Parva in the same breath," remarked Gideon.

Kenelm slanted a look at him. "That's *why* I'm a policeman."

"Okay, I'll leave it until the morning." Annie stood up. "Thanks for the coffee."

Kenelm got to his feet as well. "I'll come too."

"There's no need. I can manage."

"I'm sure you can, but I don't need to be a copper to see Calli and Gideon want to be alone. Also, I'd rather not have my landlady in jug for manslaughter if you happen to run across Violet on the way home."

"She'll be long indoors by now. Besides, it's more likely to be the other way around as soon as her letter comes back saying the rare-plant register has known all about the marsh orchid for the last two years."

"Then I'm definitely coming with you. It's been enough hassle moving once. I don't want to do it all over again because your residuary legatee is selling the house."

Annie stalked ahead on the way back, pulling the case containing her sale stock and wrapped in thought. Kenelm kept quiet. Anything he said was bound to be wrong. Not for the first time, he regretted his upbringing at Fencross Manor. His childhood companions had all been cousins or friends from school. None of the Grays had been encouraged to look beyond their boundaries. Thus stocky, truculent Annie, who had lived in Fencross

Parva almost as long as he had, was an enigma except as his cousin Lydia's friend. Even then, he suspected Lydia had mostly taken Annie up as an untidy, dark-haired foil to her own blonde perfection - and as an act of defiance to prove she couldn't be dictated to.

Gideon, on the other hand, had been a constant burr. Part family, due to being the son of an illegitimate Gray, but mostly village, he had irritated Kenelm for years with his easy freedom and his scorn for the Manor. Kenelm had been outraged when Gideon - the boy from the gardener's lodge - was sent to Harrow with him. Then furious when Gideon proved more popular. And yet they'd formed a grudging, unspoken pact there, best enemies was how Gideon described it, Fencross Parva versus the world. Now they were close to being friends. Both of them had done a lot of growing up.

Old thoughts, rat-in-trap thoughts. If he hadn't been brought up privileged and unable to talk to the common man, would he have made a better go at marriage? If Gideon hadn't been a constant, sceptical presence, would Kenelm have joined the police in a perverse wish to prove not all Grays were useless? Certainly he'd had as much unlearning as learning to do when he enrolled. Equally certainly, he was good at his job and he *liked* being good at it. But life around the edges? Not so much.

"I think I'm allergic to evenings off," he said aloud.

Annie snorted. "I know I am. I need the sales and the goodwill, but I itch whenever I'm kept from my easel for too long."

"And yet you're involved with the plants on the common."

"That's different. It's work in a way. Most of my sales come from paintings I've done there."

"But why the... what did you call them? Squares-of-care?"

"It's an ongoing survey. I record what's in each of them, take measurements, test the pH, that sort of thing. It gives a long-term health record of the common."

"Isn't it time-consuming?"

"Not really. It's soothing. It reconnects me with nature."

"And my mother does this survey too?" Kenelm had to work to keep the astonishment out of his voice.

That elicited an amused snort. "She used to. Terrific plantswoman, Dinah. I've taken over her squares now. She got me into it back when I was a stroppy teenager stomping around being cross with everything. Don't say it," she added in warning.

Kenelm bit back the comment about not much having changed. They'd reached the house anyway. He was still surprised Annie had worked so readily with his mother. He'd always had the idea that she'd curled her lip at the Manor, even more so after his dear cousin Lydia walked out on Gideon, having exhausted his usefulness, and decamped to London.

The two discontented visitors were sprawled at the kitchen table with coffee, smart phones and a mess of cake crumbs. Annie shot them a look of extreme dislike and went through to her studio with the dogs. Kenelm headed for bed. He answered emails from his sons and a longer one from Sarah which was simply a continuation of her phone call. That exacerbated the raw patch inside him to such an extent that he picked up the spy thriller he was reading. Caught up in its clever convolutions, he was only vaguely aware of doors banging downstairs, of dogs barking on the common, of the petulant couple coming to bed.

Eventually, having bludgeoned his mind into a relative calm, he shut the book and turned out the light, secure in the knowledge that he didn't have to be at the station until late morning.

CHAPTER FOUR

The ringing of Kenelm's phone and simultaneous buzzing of his police radio brought him awake far too early.

"Morning, Inspector. Still in Fencross Parva? Good, get yourself to a house called Riverdene asap. It's somewhere in Mulberry Lane. Report of a fatality. I'm sending you PC Bryce as back-up."

"Chief?" he said, groping for the bedside light.

"The same. And don't tell me you're on late shift today, you're also on the spot, so get down there and take time off in lieu."

Time off in lieu. The last great myth. "Case ref?"

"I'm sending it through now. Bryce will meet you there. 999 call was made by a neighbour, currently having hysterics if the operator is to be believed, hence the lack of house number. Once you've calmed her down it would be interesting to find out what she was doing there this early. Are you on your way yet?"

"Practically at the door, sir," lied Kenelm.

He broke the connection, swore as he showered in under a minute, shaved as he scrambled into his uniform and was reading the scant details of the call-out as he hit the kitchen.

"Kettle's just boiled," said Annie, not looking around

from scooping dog food into bowls. "No need to hurry, the visitors aren't up yet. I thought you said you were on late shift today."

"I am. Apparently I'm also on early. Where the hell is Riverdene? It's on this road somewhere."

"It's one of the ex-council semi-detached bungalows further around the corner. Just past the Clattering turn-off but on this side, opposite the care home."

Kenelm pictured Mulberry Lane in his mind. It bent sharply to the left three hundred yards up from Annie's cottage, thus enclosing the common on two sides. "Backing on to the common?" he asked.

"Unfortunately, yes. Third or fourth double-bungalow along. I can never remember which until I get there. You can't miss it. It's got a wishing well and a coven of gnomes in the front garden."

Kenelm added extra milk to cool the coffee. Annie's description didn't sound as if the occupant was a friend. "You're well-informed."

"I should be, considering I have to go past it every time I visit Mum. The old witch always manages to be in her garden emanating waves of false sympathy."

Definitely not a friend. "Which witch?" he said, and winced. "What I mean is, who lives at Riverdene?"

"That woman we were talking about last night. The one your mother and I would dearly love to run off the face of the earth, or at least out of Fencross Parva. Violet Renshaw."

It was a good thing Kenelm had trained himself years ago to freeze at moments of tension or he'd have owed Annie a new mug. As it was he finished his coffee safely and managed a preoccupied nod before leaving the house and turning left along Mulberry Lane. Around the ninety degree bend, he spotted a squad car reversing neatly into a space a little way up the Clattering road. That was efficient even by Dee's standards. He could only hope she'd been in the vicinity already when the call came through. He changed direction to meet her.

"Morning, guvnor," said Dee, leaning across to open the door for him. "Hop in. It always looks more official arriving together, rather than me swanning up in the car while you stride along behind."

"You're inappropriately cheerful for someone heading to a fatality," remarked Kenelm.

His constable gave him a sunny smile. "We're not there yet, are we? In the meantime, I've escaped a morning of entering data into the computer."

Oh God, she hadn't been in the vicinity already. "Sticking to the speed limit all the way, I trust?"

Innocence radiated from her. "I was told it was urgent, sir. Incoherent woman having hysterics all over the phone operator."

"Hmm. Turn right, then it's the bungalow with the gnomes on the left."

"You know the deceased, do you?"

"Only by repute. She had a row with my mother yesterday evening."

"Awkward," said Dee with masterly understatement. "This looks like the place. I'm told the hysterical neighbour will be inside to let us in."

The woebegone lady who answered the door of the bungalow blinked at the sight of them. "Oh," she said faintly, clutching an unlovely cat to her thin chest.

"Miss Saxon? I'm Inspector Gray and this is Constable Bryce. We're here in response to a call to the emergency services."

"I didn't know what to do," she quavered. "Such a shock. I fed Timmy. I had to. He was scratching at her door and wailing. They say animals always know, don't they?"

Kenelm was familiar with the babbling-witness

scenario. "They do indeed. Perhaps we could come in and you tell us what happened from the beginning. Better indoors than out here on the doorstep."

The word *doorstep*, with its connotation of *interested neighbours*, worked its usual charm. Moments later they were seated in a fussy lounge and Miss Saxon was explaining she lived next door and hadn't had the least idea anything was wrong until Timmy started howling in the back garden to come in.

"He always has breakfast with Violet, you see, only she calls him Mr Fluffkins, and I could tell he hadn't been fed because he didn't smell of fishy. So I knocked on her door, then I phoned, and I was a bit worried because the curtains were still drawn and she always gets up early like me, so I used my key. We have each other's keys for emergencies. I called hello, because she might have had a fall, mightn't she, and she *was* a bit giddy yesterday, but there was still no answer. So I tapped very quietly on the bedroom door, then I pushed it open and there she was, all staring and cold just like when Father went, so I fed Timmy his fishy and phoned 999. So silly of me, I called Dr Gotobed first, but of course he isn't there any more, is he? Oh dear, it's given me such a shock I don't know what I'm doing." Her voice dissolved into shaky sobs.

"That's all right," said Dee, patting the woman's arm and narrowly missing being swiped by a lightning-fast set of claws. "You stay here and we'll pop along to the bedroom and take a look."

Kenelm pulled on latex gloves and went into the hallway. Deep scratches in the paintwork of the door at the end gave a good indication of where to try first. It led to an elaborate bedroom, rank with clashing perfumes, where the late Violet Renshaw lay between rose-patterned sheets, eyes wide open, reaching out one arm as if to get to the bedside phone. Kenelm stood motionless, taking in the dried saliva around her mouth and the unnatural way her upper body was twisted.

"One for the coroner," he said. "I'll do the video and contact the station."

"There's no sign of violence or disturbance, sir," said Dee doubtfully.

"Any unexpected death has to be reported to the coroner. You get Miss Saxon inside her own house and outside a cup of tea and find out if Violet Renshaw had any underlying health conditions."

"Taking Timmy Fluffkins with us?"

"That would be a bonus. We'll want her details and anything she knows about the deceased - relatives, medical practitioner, solicitor, that sort of thing. Also both of their movements last night and this morning. There was a WI meeting in the church hall yesterday evening. Violet Renshaw attended it. I would be amazed if Miss Saxon wasn't there too."

"On it, sir." Dee returned along the hallway murmuring, "Here kitty, kitty."

Left alone, Kenelm slipped on shoe coverings, opened the window carefully to clear the air of the heavy scent, set his phone to video and did a meticulous survey of the room, making an oral commentary as he went. He'd apologise to the coroner's office later if he was wasting their time. All coppers have a sixth sense for something wrong and his was currently blowing a police whistle fit to take his head off. It wasn't the unexpectedness of the death. It wasn't the incongruity of a rigid body in a fancy, frilly bedroom. It was the look of sheer, terrified, panicking horror on the late Violet's face as she reached unavailingly for the phone.

Dee Bryce followed Miss Saxon next door. The contrast, as she was assailed by a musty, old-fashioned smell taking her right back to her gran's house before she'd had it redone, could not be greater. Like Gran's place, this old-fashioned semi-detached bungalow with its worn carpets and elderly satin-striped wallpaper, was pin neat and rigidly clean. Even before she saw the lounge, Dee knew what to expect. Sure enough, there was a wing-backed armchair on one side of the electric fire, a plain one next to it, a television in the corner and a square table by the window. There was also a strong odour of cat.

Timmy made a flying leap for the wing chair, curling up with a look on his face that dared Dee to evict him.

"They always find the most comfortable seats," said Dee, sitting on an upright chair by the table and getting out her notebook.

Miss Saxon sank into the plain armchair and regarded the malignant creature dotingly. "That used to be Father's chair."

Figures. "Have you had him long?" asked Dee.

"Oh yes, he adopted us nearly ten years ago. Such a thin little thing. Father said we could only keep him if he didn't cost anything, but he liked him really. I'd often come in from buying his baccy to find Timmy on his lap, both of them fast asleep."

"Bless. How did it come about that Mrs Renshaw fed him breakfast?"

A trace of distress crossed the faded face. Her thin fingers worked nervously. "Well, Violet didn't have a cat, you see, so she said she'd borrow him in the mornings to... to save me money and of course she gave him fishy which he does like, but it's so dear, isn't it?"

"Shocking price," agreed Dee. *Something odd there. Generosity on Violet's part? Or sneakily taking the cat over?* "I'd better get some details. What is your full name, please?"

"Minna Alexandra Saxon. Minna is Swedish. It was my grandmother's name."

"Very pretty. How long have you lived here?"

"Always."

Dee blinked. She'd never moved? Not ever? That explained the decor, then. It probably dated from her parents' marriage. "Do you live alone?"

"Since I lost Father, yes."

As ever, Dee had to repress the word *careless*. Bad Dee. Behave. "It was lucky you got along with your neighbour then."

"Oh I *did*. Father didn't like her much - he shouted at her when the men landscaping her garden played the radio loudly and drove their little digger around, disturbing him listening to the cricket. He was rude about her fence too. I think it's lovely, such a nice bright colour, and I told her so right from the beginning. She said not to worry because elderly gentlemen can often be stuck in their ways. She's been *such* a friend to me. I couldn't have managed at all without her help when Father passed away. There were so many forms, I was quite bewildered. But she knew just what to do about filling in the probate thing and getting the deeds changed from Father to me and all the other bits and pieces. I don't know what I'm going to do without her."

"I'm sure people will help if you ask. When did you last see Mrs Renshaw? Before this morning that is."

Minna looked mildly surprised. "At WI yesterday, of course. We usually go together, but this time Violet had to get to the church hall early. She had suggested the speaker, you see, so she wanted to greet her."

"Oh yes? Who was it?"

"Her name is Heather Meadows. She's well known and she writes books. She's even going to be on the television! It was so lucky she was already on the WI approved list.

There's been a little difficulty with Violet's suggestions before because the WI have to be strict about who they ask to speak, not like our gardening club which is *much* more friendly."

Dee gave a soothing murmur. "What time did Mrs Renshaw get to the hall?"

"About half past six to help Heather set up. I didn't arrive until ten to seven with everyone else. I had offered to go with Violet, but she didn't want Heather to feel too crowded. It was a shame, because I'd have liked to talk to her. There wasn't time afterwards. She had to leave early. She's doing a book tour, you see, and only fitted the WI talk in as a favour to Violet."

"That was very generous of her. Was it a good talk?" asked Dee.

"Oh *yes*," said Minna, growing animated. "It was about eating for nothing. Father would have been ever so interested. Heather made some lovely side-dishes and salads for us to try. After the meeting Violet and I walked back together and... and that was the last time I saw her." She turned damp, tragic eyes on Dee.

Dee adopted a brisk tone. "Do you know which doctor she used? Did she have any problems with her health?"

"Dr Smith. He's very young and vigorous, quite different from Dr Gotobed. I do miss him. But Calli is very nice, of course, and the library is such a boon. Our old one closed, you see and I was *distraught*. Violet thought Dr Smith was too unsympathetic to be a good doctor, but I've found him most helpful. He prescribed a rub for my ankles which is marvellous. I said to Violet only yesterday she ought to ask him for some as she seemed a bit unsteady, but she said it was only pins and needles and she'd had it before."

"When was this?"

"At the end of the meeting when we were putting on

our coats. There had been a bit of unpleasantness and I wondered if it had made her wobbly. Some people do get like that, you know. I hate it when people raise their voices. It upsets my tummy."

Unpleasantness? Hadn't the guvnor said the deceased had been arguing with his mother? "The doctor will be able to tell us, I expect. Who is your friend's next-of-kin? Did she have any adult children?"

"She said she and her husband hadn't been blessed that way. They kept hoping, but he died. It was only her and her mother at home before that, because her father had married someone else. That's why she understood about it just being Father and me. She said she and I had a special bond. Oh dear." She started sniffling again and groped in her cardigan sleeve for a damp handkerchief.

"That'll be nice to remember," cut in Dee firmly. "How about her other friends? Did she have any men friends?"

"Oh no, nothing like *that*," said Minna in a shocked voice. "It's not true at all what people said about Jerry Ellwood. He sold Violet the bungalow. It was natural he should call from time to time after she moved in to see how she was getting on. Ellwood & Smart have most of the Fencross business when people move house. He's most obliging. He valued me for probate and I didn't have to pay *anything*."

Dee made a note of the name and didn't mention that people never do pay for valuations. "Do you know which solicitor Mrs Renshaw used?"

"She said solicitors were expensive - well, of course I know they are - but it was important for everyone to make a will and it was very easy to do it yourself." Her gaze turned tragic again. "It was as if she *knew*."

Whoa. Diversion. Fast. "How about a nice cup of tea? It'll do you good."

Minna jumped up as if she'd been scalded. "Oh my,

what am I thinking of? I never offered you one. It's all been such a shock. Violet got a will form at the post office at the same time as I did, not that I've got much to leave, but I do want Timmy to be looked after and they can't do it themselves, can they?"

Dee considered Timmy Fluffkins probably could, but she gave a bright nod and followed Minna into the kitchen. The resemblance to Gran's house grew even more pronounced. Painfully tidy, with original 1950s lino on the floor and a plastic cloth on the table. An elderly fridge whirring in one corner. A twin-tub. When had Dee last seen a twin tub? Even Gran had a front-loader automatic.

Minna glanced at the tea caddy in an agony of indecision, peered into the teapot, added boiling water and replaced its knitted cosy. The contents of the fridge, Dee saw in the brief glimpse she was afforded, were meagre. A carton of milk. A single lamb chop. Two different pieces of squashed-looking cake. Half an apple pie. A newish container on the bottom shelf and - judging by the smell - a covered plate of fish. Dee strongly suspected it had come from Riverdene for the cat's breakfast.

"I'm afraid I haven't any biscuits. Violet's got some lovely ones. I could easily pop next door and..."

"Just tea is fine," said Dee, giving the unappealing beverage the benefit of the doubt. "Did you spend a lot of time with your friend?"

"Oh yes, I see her most days, saying hello over the fence if nothing else. We were in a bubble over lockdown and that was lovely because she understands computers and I could sit with her when we zoomed the gardening club meetings and the WI. Even now I have lunch or tea with her sometimes. She said to come in for lunch today. We were going to have a nice piece of quiche and finish the..." She broke off, looking stricken.

Poor old thing, thought Dee, and asked about birthdays and dentists and other soothing, mundane details.

CHAPTER FIVE

Kenelm completed his tour of Riverdene and opened the back door to a garden as well-stocked as the front one. This stretch of Mulberry Lane was higher than Annie's part, so the houses here were built on rising ground, meaning the garden fell away pleasingly towards the expanse of common. He was momentarily surprised at the length of the garden until he remembered these bungalows had been built in the days when council tenants were confidently assumed to grow their own vegetables.

Riverdene had evidently been bought from the council years ago and then sold on. Anything less like an allotment - or indeed less like the conventional grass rectangle next door, bordered sparsely by daffodils, crocus and meagre shrubs - would be hard to imagine.

For a start, the three sides of Violet Renshaw's picket fence had been painted in various shades of purple. Within them, flower beds curved in and belled out, gay with spring bulbs, primula and forsythia. A gravel path wound past a circular lawn on one side to a small pond on the other, ending at a gate which gave on to the common. Kenelm, walking down the path to check the bolt on the gate, reflected that it was the garden of a woman with a lot of time on her hands. He could see why she'd been president of the gardening club.

The only jarring note was the bed by the pond where straggly, aromatic shrubs masked a tangle of low greenery. Even here someone had been working, judging by the recent boot marks trampled across the surface. Except... Kenelm bent to inspect them more closely. The shoes in Violet Renshaw's wardrobe had been a dainty size four. These had been made by something much larger.

Cold sheeted over him. He knew these boot prints. He'd been seeing them in the mud around Annie's chicken coops every day this past fortnight. He stared across the corner of the common to where those same chicken coops rose above the line of her fence. What the merry hell had Annie Dearlove been doing in the garden of a woman she hated? And when?

The advisable procedure at this juncture would be to excuse himself from the case on the grounds of personal interest. The reasons why he wasn't stopped him dead. First, Gideon would never forgive him. Annie and Gideon went back a long way. It would be as if Kenelm had thrown his cousin's oldest friend to the wolves. The second reason was Annie herself. Yes, she was combative and outspoken and inclined to view the world as her enemy. But she'd taken him in when he was too emotionally raw to think straight. She'd given him space and left him alone. Anger she certainly had, seething away in bucket loads, but so did he at the moment. Despite that, she'd helped him when she didn't have to, which made her perilously close to a comrade.

These thoughts raced through his mind, leaving him appalled and confounded. He, who'd always prided himself on his detachment, was putting friendship above his job. He mechanically checked the lock and the bolt on the gate, noted that the sagging wire netting surrounding Miss Saxon's garden next door was derisory as far as secure perimeter fencing was concerned, and that a four-foot dividing fence was no bar at all to a determined intruder, and went back to the house to finish his report. By concentrating hard, he managed to push away the memory of Annie and his mother having to be restrained just last evening from offering violence to the woman now lying lifeless further down the hall.

The reply from the station had come through by the time Dee returned. "I've escaped from Minna Saxon," she said. "Do you want to interview her?"

"Not yet, unless there's anything new she told you?"

"I've taken it all down. Violet had no close relatives, as far as Minna knows. Possible covert gentleman friend in the past - my interpretation - but not recently. She was a little unsteady yesterday, but had no underlying health problems. She was registered with Dr Smith here in Fencross Parva and with a dentist in Ely. Minna has no idea about the solicitor, they got will forms from the post office together."

"Cosy."

"What's the score here?"

"Van to remove the deceased is due any moment, then we seal the place and wait for orders. I *imagine* those orders will be to unseal the door again and go through her paperwork looking for an official contact number."

"No point going back to the station then," said Dee. "We'll get half way to Ely and have to turn around. Got any decent coffee at your gaff?"

Kenelm wasn't anywhere near ready to face Annie yet. "My gaff is infested with Airbnb visitors, none of whom I want to see me in uniform."

"Pity. It's too early for the pub to be open and we'll be mobbed if we go to the nice deli on Church Parade. Calli's place?"

Where Calli was these days, Gideon wasn't far away, and Gideon was old-Fencross. He'd see the implications of Violet Renshaw's death even faster than Kenelm had. Also, both Calli and Gideon were avid detective-novel readers so they were bound to dive straight into a well of speculation about her demise. On the other hand, they'd keep it to themselves and it would give Kenelm time to consider his approach to Annie. "Plan," he agreed. "We'll leave the car here and walk. We won't attract so much attention."

Calli had just put the coffee maker on and was unenthusiastically contemplating a spot of gardening when the kitchen door opened.

"Morning," said Dee Bryce cheerfully. "That smells good. I tried the library door but it was shut. I can go away again if you're busy."

"Hello," said Calli, pleased. She'd got to know Dee quite well during the murder investigation in Fencross Parva last month, well enough for the young constable to have adopted the old-Fencross habit of using the back door. "Come in. What are you doing here? Social call? Or whiling away the time waiting for Kenelm?"

"Strictly speaking, I'm working. I'm not really here, but I need something to take away the taste of Minna Saxon's tea. The guvnor might be here, depending on whether he's supposed to be on shift or not."

"You've lost me," said Calli.

Kenelm Gray followed his constable in. "Ignore her. Desist, Bryce. If you happened to be offering coffee, Calli, I wouldn't say no. I'd also like to ask if you know anything about Minna Saxon or Violet Renshaw."

Calli fetched two more mugs from the cupboard as her visitors divested themselves of coats and hats and sat down at the kitchen table. *Minna and Violet? What was going on here?* "A bit. Not a lot. You heard most of what I know from Annie last night. Minna is a library member with a passion for billionaire romances and Westerns with a strong, silent hero. She is said to be under Violet's thumb. Violet isn't a library member, so I don't know her at all. Why are you interested?"

"Because in the interval between last night and this morning, Violet died and Minna found her."

Calli stared at him in astonishment. "Good heavens. Was that why Minna rang here first thing this morning and then rang off again in a fluster? I don't understand. Violet was fine yesterday. Was she ill?"

"Not according to Minna," said Dee, adding sugar to her mug. "The doctor may know differently."

"Crikey." Calli struggled to take it in. That fussy, powder puff of a woman, gone. A disquieting thought struck her. "Why are you involved? Was it a break in? Was she attacked? Please tell me there aren't burglars in the village."

Kenelm spoke quickly. "Nothing like that. She was in bed, house locked up, no mess or disturbance. The coroner has to be informed of any unexpected death. They'll do a post-mortem and find the cause. Meanwhile, I'm waiting for orders."

Why wait here? Why not at Violet's bungalow or in Annie's kitchen? Calli took in the tense set of Kenelm's shoulders, his slightly distanced demeanour. "You don't think it was natural, do you? It's okay, you can talk. The library's empty. I did open first thing for the school-run parents, but an appalling couple came in wanting a graphic, eye-witness tour of where Norman Seaton was killed last month and what did he look like and could I lie down exactly where I found him and..."

"Yuk," said Dee.

"Precisely, so I hustled them out and closed up."

"The guvnor's got an itch about Violet's death," explained Dee. "I have too. It was the way she was reaching for the phone like someone in a horror-film trailer. Mind you, she could have simply remembered some instruction she'd forgotten to give one of her friends. Reading between the lines of Minna's conversation, it sounds as if she was a right bossy boots."

"She was certainly lording it over the gardening club members yesterday. I do remember Uncle Matthew saying Minna Saxon swapped one tyrant for another when her father died. That must be what he meant. Poor Minna. I wonder if she's ever had a life of her own?"

Dee pursed her lips. "I wouldn't say so from talking to her. Classic spinster-daughter-carer. All her furniture dates from the ark. She won't have chosen any of it herself. Still, at least she'll reclaim full custody of Timmy the cat, who is another tyrant by the looks of it. Incidentally, guvnor, there's a plate of fish for the cat in Minna's fridge that I suspect she liberated from Violet's place before we arrived."

"Proof?" asked Kenelm.

"Very posh pair of plates - which are the newest thing in the fridge by thirty years apart from a tub of something or other - and I don't think she can afford fish."

"I'm sure she can't," said Calli. "God knows what she lives on. I don't charge her a subscription."

The kitchen door opened again and Gideon came in. "And that," he said, dropping a kiss on her head, "is why your library will never make a profit. Minna has a tiny pension that the insurance firm her father worked for organised for all their employees."

Calli smiled up at him, her heart lifting. "Naturally you'd know that. Does it cover her rent?"

"There isn't any rent. Her father bought the bungalow from the council for a song when there was that government push to encourage private ownership. Then he kept Minna even harder-up, claiming he needed all the spare cash to pay for it. Strangely, it didn't affect his account at the off-licence."

"He certainly didn't spend anything on the house," said Dee. "She's still got the original lino in the kitchen."

Calli met her eyes in agreement. "Did you see the twin tub? It should be in a museum."

Gideon turned to Kenelm. "I could smell the coffee," he said. "I'm not being nosy."

"Like hell you aren't," retorted his cousin. "If someone hasn't told you by now that there's been a squad car outside Riverdene bungalow all morning, then this village is losing its touch."

"Half-a-dozen people may have mentioned it. Go on then. Spill the beans. No point having a policeman in the family and not getting the inside gen."

"Violet Renshaw. Alive and kicking yesterday. Found by Minna Saxon dead in bed in the act of reaching for the phone this morning. Satisfied?"

"This would be the same Violet who..."

"Yes, yes, the same Violet whom both my mother and your friend Annie wanted to pulverise to a jelly last night. Amusing, isn't it?"

Gideon poured himself a coffee and leaned against the work top. "If it was obviously foul play, you wouldn't be sitting around here, you'd be organising forensic tents and police tape."

"I remember," said Calli with feeling. "Kenelm says it wasn't a break-in."

Gideon raised his eyebrows. "And she evidently *wasn't* pulverised to a jelly, yet you're not happy."

Kenelm gave an irritable sigh. "No, I'm not. She was terrified of something just before she died and I want to know what. However, it isn't up to me. If the post-mortem comes back clear, then we unseal the place, let the appropriate people know and forget the whole thing.

No reason for you two to repeat your amateur detective techniques."

But Calli, thinking about poor downtrodden Minna and all the bustling, inquisitive women at WI last night, was troubled. "I don't think it's that simple. You realise Minna Saxon is going to tell everyone who calls around with a spare portion of casserole or an unwanted tin of cat food, that when she found her, Violet's expression was frightened?"

"There's probably a queue of neighbours at her door already," agreed Gideon. "The rumour mills will go into overdrive."

"They will anyway," said Dee. "Human nature. The fact that on the surface it all looks natural is neither here nor there. Suspicion will fall on whoever has a key - or anyone who could have obtained a key."

Gideon's lips tightened. Calli knew what he was thinking. *Not again. Not in my village.* "It makes for a foul atmosphere," he said. "When will you know the result of the post-mortem?"

Kenelm spread his hands. "How long is a piece of string? Could be today, could be tomorrow, maybe the weekend. It all depends on how busy they are, how many people are off sick, the rank of the investigating officers screaming at them about other cases and how close they're getting to a target deadline."

"Meanwhile your hands are tied. Where does that leave Fencross Parva?"

"It leaves it exactly where it was yesterday," said Kenelm.

"No, it doesn't."

"Damn you, Gideon. No, of course it doesn't. It leaves it with a nasty taste at the back of its throat. It leaves it remembering last night's WI meeting and any other time the deceased has made herself unpopular. It leaves it full of rumours and suspicions."

"The idea of either Annie or your mother having anything to do with her death is laughable," said Gideon flatly.

"That won't stop people talking behind their backs if they were the last people to have furious arguments with her."

Dee was studiously drinking her coffee, pretending not to hear her boss taking a personal interest in the case. Calli didn't blame her. She watched the two men, their expressions fleetingly alike, and knew exactly what was coming next.

"It strikes me," said Gideon, "whatever the post-mortem comes up with, we are back in action if only to scotch any gossip. We need to find out what happened."

Oh, Gideon, I do love you.

"Don't look at me," replied Kenelm. "I can't stop you asking questions, but Dee and I have to follow orders. If we are told to leave well alone and go and direct traffic in Ely because some idiot has jammed his lorry under the railway bridge again, then that's what we do."

"Sure you do. But just supposing Calli and I invite you around for a meal, we can't talk about *nothing*, can we?"

"That would be plain rude, guvnor," said Dee. She winked at Calli.

Kenelm's phone buzzed. "What do you know," he said, thumbing the screen. "Over to Riverdene and go through all the paperwork we can find." He stood, shrugging into his coat "Thanks for the coffee."

Dee sprang up too, settling her regulation bowler with a firm tug. "Much appreciated."

At the door, Kenelm glanced back. His look held exasperation, laced through with the tiniest trace of relief. "So, what time's dinner?"

CHAPTER SIX

Leaving Calli's house with the suspicion that she and Gideon were already working on a timetable, Kenelm realised what had subconsciously irritated him about his cousin when they were growing up was how Gideon - the boy from the Lodge - cared in his bones about Fencross Parva, how he assumed he had the *right* to care, whereas Kenelm - who should have had that right by virtue of his family living at the Manor - had merely taken the village for granted. He was disgusted at himself.

Marvellous. Now he was unsettled *and* full of self-loathing. This was turning into a splendid day. Striding past Hope Cottage, he noticed the visitors' car had departed. He squared his shoulders. He might as well have the chat with Annie now since it couldn't possibly make him feel any worse. "I need to pick my charger up," he said, turning down the side path.

Dee followed without comment, crouching to make a fuss of Sofi and Star who set up a cacophony of welcome-home barking as soon as he opened the kitchen door. Their madly-wagging tails and air of doggy joy at seeing him put an unexpected dent in his bad mood. *Cheers, guys, make it easy for me why don't you?*

"Aren't you both gorgeous?" crooned Dee. "I'd love a

dog, but it wouldn't be fair with a small house and me and Eithan out all day and the kids at school."

"Oh, it's you," said Annie, coming downstairs with an armful of bedding. "I thought it was the damn guests back again."

And suddenly it was easy. Gideon believed in Annie implicitly. Kenelm had seen too much during his time in the force to go that far, but he trusted his cousin's judgement as far as character was concerned. That meant he had to clear this up. He waited for her to start the washing machine and then said, "I was in Violet Renshaw's garden this morning."

Annie made a face. "I did wonder when you asked where Riverdene was. Has the evil witch made a complaint?"

A complaint about what? Not good. Not good at all. Kenelm sensed Dee sinking quietly to the floor to sit with the dogs. He spoke as if he hadn't noticed, feeling his way. "Annie, the prints of your boots are all over her flower bed."

"Only the corner by the pond," objected Annie. "I was careful not to tread on any of her flowers."

"Going to tell me how they came to be there?"

"Bloody visitors let the dogs out after you went to bed. Apparently they fancied a romantic stroll on the common by moonlight. I'd just come through from the studio, so naturally the hounds were out of the back door the moment it opened."

"You let the dogs out in the evenings anyway."

"I don't let them on to the common. And I make quite sure that damn cat of Minna's isn't sitting on the fence taunting them."

Now Kenelm remembered a cat's yowl and the dogs barking last night. "What happened?"

"What do you think happened? They gave chase. The cat streaked over the footbridge straight into Minna's garden, then scrambled over the fence into Violet's, followed by Sofi and Star barking their fool heads off. I'm surprised you didn't hear them."

"I did. I'd forgotten."

"Yes, well, I jammed on my head torch and wellies and ran after them. The bloody cat was perched on the fence above the pond. Sofi had got into Violet's garden, Star was still in Minna's. I climbed across Minna's flattened netting and hoisted myself over the dividing fence, heaved Sofi *back* over the fence, which was no mean feat, scrambled back into Minna's garden myself, clipped on the dogs' leads, straightened the netting and was all set to bring the hounds home via the road when Violet opened her back door and said in a sweet, carrying voice that there was nothing to see in her garden and if I came one step further she'd report me for trespassing. I didn't mention I'd already been in and out. I just said the dogs had escaped and I was taking them home. To which she replied that if they'd upset Mr Fluffkins she'd have them put down. She then stood there in her kitchen doorway eating her plate of supper one-handed while I walked Sofi and Star all the way up Minna's side path and out to the road. I expect she went through to the front room to keep a beady eye on me as far as the corner. I swear I could feel daggers poised at my back."

"And she was all right, was she?"

"Violet? She was in stunning form. Why?"

"Because this morning, she's just the tiniest bit dead."

Annie stared. "You're joking."

Was that genuine astonishment? Kenelm thought it was. Something uncommonly like relief threaded through him. "I'm not. That's why I was called out first thing."

"What of?"

"We don't know. She was in bed. Minna Saxon let herself in when she didn't answer the door or the phone and found her."

She straightened. "I'd better go through all that again for the record then."

"No need," said Dee from the floor where she was covered in golden retrievers and writing in her notebook. "I've got it down. I just need the timings, any witnesses, then I'll type it up and you can sign it."

Kenelm glanced down. "Oh, very regulation. Use the clothes-brush in the mud room before you go back out in public. What time was it, Annie? Can you remember?"

"It wasn't late, because I was in bed before midnight. Elevenish or just after, I guess."

"Funny time for her to be eating supper."

"Not really. I often have a late sandwich if I've been working."

"She hadn't been working. She'd been at a meeting."

Annie shrugged. "So? She was greedy. Everyone knew that. As for witnesses, I didn't see anyone, but someone might remember the dogs barking. I did consider asking her to speak up because I wasn't sure they'd heard her on the other side of the road. Maybe I should have done."

"Must be the first time you've held back. How about the visitors from here? The ones who opened the gate to the common in the first place?"

"They went off in the opposite direction. Didn't want to see the chaos they'd caused, blast them. Out of sight, out of mind."

"Right. Thanks. We'll leave you in peace and look through her paperwork for the next-of-kin. Ready, Dee?"

"Yes, sir. Charger, sir?"

Kenelm eyed her. "That tone of voice is borderline insubordination."

"Sorry, sir. Won't happen again."

And that was a lie if ever he'd heard one.

Calli finished her coffee and looked at Gideon. He hadn't moved since Kenelm and Dee had left. "What are you thinking?" *As if she couldn't guess.*

"I'm thinking about Kenelm not being satisfied with Violet Renshaw's death."

"Neither he nor Dee really explained why. Just that she looked frightened, which she would if she'd woken suddenly and found she was having a severe asthma attack or a stroke or something."

"It's got to be more than that. I've known Kenelm all my life. The boy from the Lodge and the boy from the Manor. We were thrown together unwillingly, but that doesn't mean I didn't respect his good qualities even while I was resenting them. He likes to know things. He likes things to be right. If he's got a hunch about this, it'll be justified."

"Then the post-mortem will find something, the police will open a case and set up an investigation."

"I hope they do it properly. That's the other thing about Kenelm. Laziness infuriates him. You remember what happened with the library. He's not a detective, but when the senior investigating officer was going in the wrong direction - the easy direction - Kenelm was like a man with an abscess. He rarely shows his feelings, he never lets out the pain when he's hurting, but he frets on the inside. It's not good for him. He's got enough stress already with him and Sarah breaking up, he doesn't need more."

Calli felt a rush of love for this impossible man. "There you go again, trying to fix the world. Kenelm's not the only one who gets abscesses. He frets if things aren't right. You fret if there's something wrong in the village. You *are* old-Fencross. People come to you or Lady Honoria when stuff goes wrong, not to Sir Rollo."

"Rollo's a buffoon. Even Lady H says so and he's her son." He drummed his fingers indecisively on the table.

"Sorry. Kenelm has got me fidgety. There might not be a crime to solve like last time, but I want to do *something*. Annie and Dinah had a very public argument with Violet yesterday evening. People are going to talk about that, regardless of how trivial the subject matter might seem to be. I don't like whispers and rumours, even if they then peter out. I want to be ahead of the game."

"If there is a game."

"If there is a game."

Calli considered him. They might not have been lovers for very long, but they'd been friends for over a year. Even so, every time she thought she was getting to know him, there was another byway to travel. "You want to show solidarity, is that the idea? Shall we call on Annie then, all jolly and cheerful as if there's nothing wrong? Stroll down the road perfectly easy and carefree for the whole village to see. Just another day."

He hesitated. "She won't thank us if she's working."

"She won't be. She said she was taking a painting across to the rectory this morning. Rev Robin bought one at last night's WI meeting."

Gideon's face cleared. "Genius. I've got Bunty's furniture designs in the workshop. Give me five minutes to pick them up and we can catch Annie at the rectory if she's not at home."

Far from being grateful, Annie greeted them at her garden gate with deep suspicion. "What are you doing here?"

Calli fought to keep a straight face. "Gideon's on his way to see Bunty and I remembered your painting that Rev Robin bought. Also, I didn't know whether Kenelm had told you about Violet Renshaw."

Annie's scowl turned into a wry smile. "Come right out with it, why don't you?"

"What, you don't have friends?" said Calli. "It's what

they're for. Crikey, my pal Meriel would have been banging on the door before I was even awake if I'd had a public row with a dead woman the evening before she was found. Yes, I know she wasn't dead then. Be quiet."

"It's better than that," replied Annie. "I had another argument with her at eleven o'clock last night. I've just been making a statement for Kenelm."

"Fantastic, Annie," said Gideon. "Dig yourself a nice deep pit while you're at it. Tell us about this argument on the way to the rectory."

Rev Robin was busy with a parishioner when they arrived but Bunty was promisingly appreciative of the painting. This was the first time Calli had met the celebrated garden designer properly and she was inclined to like what she saw.

"If Robin hadn't already nabbed this for her study, I'd have it in the lounge," said Bunty. "I'll have to come over to your studio and have a browse. We're opening up the rooms here, but there was such a lack of colour when we moved in, I despaired. Reverend Silver must have had his mind on a tremendously higher plane because you wouldn't credit anyone could live in so much gloom without wanting to do something about it. Let's see the designs, Gideon. I don't think Robin will be long."

She spread them out on the table and was inspecting them with decisive nods of approval when the study door opened.

"Thank you so much," said a tremulous voice. "I did wonder, but the service last week was very good, and you've kept the old hymns which is such a comfort, so I thought I would. Violet was shocked when we heard about your appointment and didn't really think you... but we must move with the times, mustn't we, and I always *have* come along to see dear Reverend Silver for guidance. And of course the bishop can't be wrong, can he?"

"I hope not," said Rev Robin with a smile. "I'm glad I was able to help."

"Oh, you did. I feel much better."

"Hello, Minna," said Calli.

"Hello dear. I'm sorry I disturbed you this morning. So silly of me. I dialled the number for Dr Gotobed without thinking. Father always said I didn't have the sense I was born with. I was just talking to the vicar. I felt I had to."

Poor Minna. Calli felt a jab of annoyance at the late Mr Saxon for constantly belittling his daughter. "That was very clever of you. No one better. It must have been a horrible shock."

"It *was*. Especially as yesterday evening was really quite awkward, what with..." Minna saw Annie and floundered to a stop. She settled for a wavering query about how Annie's dear mother was and how she missed their little chats.

"Some days are better than others," said Annie.

Minna's face puckered in distress. "Oh, I am sorry. I admired Margaret so much when we were girls. She was terribly popular, you know, and always so gay and *alive*. She was kind too. She'd always give me a spare pencil when I lost mine and let me have her lunch when she wasn't hungry. Shall I go and see her, dear? It's only just across the road, so it's no trouble. I'd like to. I don't mind if she doesn't remember me. I can talk about the old days anyway."

"Thanks," said Annie gruffly. "She'd like that."

"I wanted to before, but Violet said..." Minna broke off in some confusion and asked lamely how the dear doggies were, then noticed the clock with the air of a drowning woman catching sight of the RNLI. "Oh dear, I've been longer than I thought. I'm going to Pat's for lunch. She phoned this morning and invited me. People are being so kind."

"People are being ghouls," corrected Annie after Minna had hurried off.

"At least she gets lunch out of it," said Calli. "Which Pat? Do I know her?"

"You must do. It'll be Pat Williams. Militant type. She's got a gorgeous Afghan hound that goes everywhere with her."

"Ah, Rupert's owner. Yes, of course I know her. She asked me if well-behaved dogs were allowed in the library. I said I didn't see why not, and he really is good. He lies down under the radiator and goes to sleep while Pat changes her book. The carpet needs hoovering afterwards though."

"Pat is another of the belladonna club. Rival faction. She used to argue non-stop with Mum when she was the president years ago before the foraging rift. It wouldn't surprise me if she argued with Violet too. Sparring for dominance. The club is famous for it."

Calli looked at her in consternation. "But they were all full of togetherness last night."

Annie snorted. "They were at a WI meeting, weren't they? Unity in opposition, no matter how much you dislike each other as a general rule."

"Unspoken treaty of offence and defence," agreed Gideon. "It's worked for Kenelm and me for years."

"I sometimes think I've spent the last twelve months in my own world," said Calli ruefully. "I don't know any of this, only what people talk about in the library. It looks as though Lady H was right. I do need to get out more."

Annie directed a comradely glance at her. "It's such a pain, isn't it, the way she's aristocratically overbearing and always bang on?"

"Are you talking about Lady Honoria?" said Rev Robin. "That woman is terrifying. I had to remind myself she was just another lamb in my flock when I was introduced to her."

There was a considering silence. "No," said Calli, shaking her head slowly. "No, I can't make the image come right, Robin. Sorry."

Gideon smiled. "Lady H has her human moments. How are you so well up with the belladonna ladies, Annie? You said you were never darkening their doors again."

"True, and I haven't. But I have to talk about *something* to Mum when I visit and there's always enough gossip swirling around the Church Parade shops to supply conversation for half an hour. Every now and again she surprises me by knowing who I'm talking about."

Underneath the words there was an edge of unhappiness. Calli saw Robin pick up on it.

Gideon saw it too. "I'll leave the designs with you, Bunty. Let me know what you think. I'm happy to alter them to suit. Better go, got a client due. Coming, Calli?"

"Sure. See you, Annie."

As they left, Rev Robin was reaching for her tablet and saying in a practical voice, "What's your mum's name? I'll be able to tell her I've bought one of your paintings when I go on my next care-home visit. Talking of which, I can't wait to get this beauty up on the wall. Please tell me you've brought all the fixings with you? I'm the world's worst at d-i-y. Bunty despairs of me."

"That's a nice woman," said Gideon once they were outside and walking slowly back.

"Yes," said Calli. "I told you how she exorcised the library for me, didn't I? Poor Minna, though. That story about Annie's mum giving her own lunch to her when they were young. Do you think she's ever not been hungry?"

Gideon's mouth twisted. "No. Never not hungry. Never not bullied. If there is any justice at all, there will be a special circle of hell reserved for people like her father."

CHAPTER SEVEN

"The laptop's got a password lock, but there's a desk and shelving in the dining room," said Kenelm. "We'll start there and hope Violet kept next-of-kin details in hard copy." He pulled on disposable gloves, took down the first box file and passed the second to Dee. "Note the contents, keep out anything important, put the rest back as you found it."

His constable nodded, seated herself on one side of the table and got to work. "Household bills. My favourite," she said in accents that sounded anything but thrilled." She riffled through the bundles. "Looks as if she's kept them for the whole six years she's lived here."

"No one ever said a policeman's lot was a happy one." He opened up his own box to discover the late Violet's financial statements, neatly divided into years. "We'll give it our best shot for an hour and then break for lunch."

By one o'clock, they knew the running costs of the house, the local firm she'd hired to remodel the garden, where the deeds were, the mini-cab company she used, her preferred supermarket, her favourite clothing, home furnishings and chocolate stores... but were no nearer finding a relative or a will.

"Or anything beyond six years ago," sad Dee. "That must be in the boxes on the next shelf."

"No, that's notes for her pamphlets. Archive stuff could be in the wardrobe or a suitcase under the bed or even in the loft."

"Fun," said Dee. "Did you mention lunch?"

"Which will also be fun. I was thinking in view of yesterday's dust-up at the Women's Institute, I might drop in on my mama for soup and a sandwich. Get her take on Violet, enjoy a smidgen of character assassination and find out what she was doing between nine pm last night and seven am this morning in case of complications."

Dee nodded. "Makes sense. Do you need me there? Only I noticed a café over the road."

"The *Cosy Kettle*?" said Kenelm, startled. "Opposite the entrance to the common? That couldn't be less you if it tried."

"It would be right up my gran's street, though. And that being the case, it will be exactly the sort of place Minna Saxon would like if she could afford it. I'm betting the customers in there will be full of gossip about the late Violet. Every little helps, as they say."

"Good thinking. Very good thinking. Well done. Reconvene back here in an hour."

He locked up and strode down Mulberry Lane towards the Manor, wondering how much longer it would be before Dee Bryce applied for a transfer to the plain clothes branch. He'd miss her. He rather thought she was good for him.

His mother was delighted to see him, confining herself to a single plaintive murmur that he should have let her know, because it was only cream of chicken and here she was all untidy from the garden.

"Spur of the moment decision. You look as elegant as always." And because he could see she was desperate to ask and he'd never get any sense out of her until she did, he added, "I haven't heard from Sarah since yesterday, but she and the boys are fine."

"Such a shame, dear. It's happening so much, isn't it?"

Strangely, that doesn't make it any easier. "Yes, but it's better to stop before everything gets too unhappy. How are you? How was your WI meeting last night? Was it an interesting talk?"

As he'd hoped, this diverted her nicely. "The *talk* was all right, dear. It was afterwards that was the trouble. That dreadful common little woman..." She broke off and turned to Kenelm's father. "Am I allowed to say common, Jolyon?"

"In the privacy of your own dining room, yes. Outside, not so much."

"Why common?" asked Kenelm, entertained despite himself.

His mother's eyes snapped. "I don't know what else you'd call someone who steals from books and puts whole passages in her pamphlets as if they were her own."

"A plagiarist," replied Kenelm. "Which book did she steal from?"

"Culpepper, of all people. Can you believe it? Only the best known historical herbal there is. So stupid."

Jolyon Gray looked quizzical. "I would have thought Culpepper's language was too dated for her to get away with it."

"Of course it is. That's what alerted me. She handed out some of her horrid little pamphlets soon after she moved here and I said it looked exactly like Nicholas Culpepper's text and she said yes, he's very good, isn't he? To which I replied that if you use extracts from another source, you have to get permission and acknowledge it in print and she said that didn't matter because he was dead. She was completely unrepentant."

Kenelm didn't dare look at his father. "Shocking."

"Well, it is," said his mother crossly, "because Culpepper wasn't entirely accurate in his medicinal uses, however satisfied they were with him in the seventeenth century, poor things. And then there was the belladonna incident, of course. So irresponsible. Anyway, I was expecting last night's speaker to be dire because Violet had recommended her."

"But she wasn't?"

"No, it was astonishing. She knew her subject and gave a good talk. I was pleasantly surprised."

"Is that Heather Meadows? She's asked Annie to illustrate her next book."

"*Has* she? Well, that shows she's a woman of sense. I shall have to buy it. Do have some of the bread, I'm sure you aren't eating enough."

He took some, then said casually, "What did you do after you came back from the meeting?"

"Really, darling, what do I ever do? Had a cup of coffee with your father, watched a documentary about the Amazon and went to bed."

"Kenelm?" said his father quietly.

They'd have to know soon. "Some time between having an argument with Annie at eleven o'clock last night and failing to feed the next-door cat at seven this morning, Violet Renshaw ceased to play any further part in Fencross Parva's affairs."

"Good," said his mother. "She'd probably been dosing herself with her own remedies. Serve her right."

"Dinah!"

She calmly lifted another spoonful of soup to her lips. "I do hope you aren't expecting me to pretend a sorrow I don't feel, Jolyon. The woman was a pest. I suppose Honoria will insist we go to the funeral. What a bore. What was it, her heart? I always distrust people who say they have to be careful with their weight and then take easily the largest piece of cake."

"Annie mentioned she was greedy."

"I was so cross, because I was trying to cut them all equally, then Pat Williams distracted me by prodding the green velvet cake in that irritating way she has and asking about additives - as if I'd know - and I miscalculated."

"The cause of death hasn't been ascertained yet. Who was her next-of-kin?"

"I don't have a clue, darling. Poor Minna Saxon might know."

"She doesn't."

His mother looked mildly intrigued. "That does surprise me. In that case, Violet had a reason for not telling her."

"I expect we'll find out. Why does everyone call her 'poor Minna'?"

"Not quite all there. I expect you saw that. And... well, there's no harm in her and I daresay it's not her fault as her dreadful father kept her terribly short of money her whole life, which is why Honoria always insists we give her our mending to do, but she does have a tiny tendency to help herself to things. Nothing big, a tube of sweets in the shop, a biscuit for later when she's out to tea, comes back a second time for an extra piece of cake at WI pretending it was her first, that sort of thing. Everybody affects not to notice. It's only tiresome people like Bonita Ellwood who declare loudly that they've put out exactly twelve teaspoons as soon as Minna strays into sight. Really, the world would be a much more pleasant place if only people were nice to each other."

This time, Kenelm did exchange a glance with his father. "Never change, Mama," he murmured.

Dee opened the café door to a little tinkle of the bell and wondered what was biting the guvnor this time. She'd got used to the constant anger eating away at him due to his marriage breaking up. It made him more than normally sarcastic, but she could cope with that. Sarcasm in the force was common currency and the guvnor's upmarket variety tickled her. She liked working with him, he was bloody good at his job and a total professional. He'd never mention personal problems to her, for instance, nor would she expect him to. It didn't mean she wouldn't facilitate anything he might have going if it would help. To which end, she'd usually be the one reminding *him* about lunch. He'd work right through otherwise. But today he'd suggested food without any of the hints she had ready. This death was bothering him. Because it was on his home turf? Because his mum and his landlady were involved? Or because it wasn't properly a case yet?

Inside the café she'd intended finding a table out of the way where she could observe and listen to the room, though that was always tricky in uniform. Instead she accidentally made eye contact with Suzy Emmet as soon as she walked in. This was what came from not concentrating. *Constant vigilance, Dee.* Then again, Suzy looked a world away from the pale, strained woman she'd encountered during the last Fencross Parva case. It wasn't surprising she'd almost not recognised her.

"Hello," said Suzy, beaming.

"Hi," she replied, accepting the inevitable. "I'm just grabbing a bite to eat. How are you?"

"I'm good. We're having a treat," said Suzy. "Do you know Mrs Candour? The kids and I live with her at Lavender House now. I still do my cleaning jobs, but it means I'm there if she needs me. She's been visiting a friend in the care home and fancied Welsh rarebit for lunch. Mrs C, this is PC Bryce who was so lovely to me about Wayne." A shadow passed over her face as she said the name of her abusive ex-husband.

"Pleased to meet you," said Dee, shaking hands. "Welsh rarebit sounds just what I'm after. Is it good here?"

"Smashing," said the bright-eyed elderly lady, patting the seat next to her. "They always do it nicely. Takes me right back to when the tennis club used to hold dances at the pavilion and we'd come home in the small hours with our shoes in ribbons and have cheese on toast and cocoa before turning in."

Suzy smiled at her fondly. "We'll have to get you on *Strictly*. Who do you fancy for a partner? I'd have Kai. He's so tall and strong and protective."

"Oh no, I'll have the young blond one with the hips and the sexy smile. Just like the boys from the tennis club. It seems a long time ago now. I don't miss the tennis so much, but I can't eat cheese at night any more. Internals won't cope with it. Don't grow old, girls, that's my advice. It takes all the fun out of life."

"My gran says that," said Dee, sitting down and hanging her hat on the back of the chair. "I always tell her it's better than the alternative."

Mrs Candour gave a chuckle. "She's a lucky woman. You're the policewoman working with Dinah Gray's second son, aren't you? I suppose you're in the village on account of Violet Renshaw. Is it true, what Minna Saxon's been saying? That Violet was frightened to death? I would have thought she was too hard-boiled for that. Like an aniseed ball, which you young things won't remember. You sucked at them and sucked at them and all they did was get smaller and harder and less appetising."

Well played, Fencross. Rumour mills hard at it already. "Inspector Gray is my guvnor, yes. That's why we're here. We're going through Mrs Renshaw's papers trying to find her next-of-kin. I don't suppose you know who it might be, do you?"

"The doctor will," said Suzy. "You have to put it in your records when you register. I had to ask him whether it was my Shannon now I'm separated. Trouble is, she's only nine, so I've given my mum's name too."

"Shannon's a good girl. I like having your children around the place. I'd forgotten how much energy they bring to an old house." Mrs Candour shook her head dubiously. "I don't think I'll ever get the hang of Harry's computer games though."

"Don't," groaned Dee. "My twins are six and they're shockers for them. I am so not a natural mother. Did Violet Renshaw have any grown-up children? I can't imagine she had many kids visiting, judging by the all the knick-knacks."

"Didn't know her," said Suzy. "Sorry."

"You didn't miss much," replied Mrs Candour. "You could ask in the care home. A lot of them spend all their time staring out of the windows. They'd see visitors. Or Bessie in here might know. Violet had only lived in Fencross a matter of a few years. Started off by poisoning the choirboys at St Athelm one Sunday. Dinah Gray called the gardening club the belladonna club after that. I must have known Dinah for fifty years and I still can never make up my mind whether she's got a wicked sense of humour or is actually serious."

Dee grinned. "I bet Mrs Renshaw didn't appreciate it."

"She didn't. Muttered behind her back to her little coterie. Violet attracted a certain type, if you know what I mean. Your best source for next-of-kin would be poor Minna Saxon if you can get any sense out of her. She was on her way to talk to the vicar when we saw her earlier, so she might be a bit calmer by now."

"We've asked. She doesn't know either," said Dee. "Never mind. It'll be in the paperwork somewhere. This looks like your food arriving. Smells awesome. I must..." She stopped as not two but three plates of Welsh rarebit were put on the table.

"I heard you," said a sprightly, middle-aged woman who was presumably Bessie. "If you're after knowing about Violet Renshaw, she was the sort who always had to be queen bee. I had her pegged the first day she came in. She chose a table where she could see the whole room, watched all the ladies and made her choice of where to stumble on her way out. Next thing you know, she's having a second cuppa with them and exchanging addresses."

Mrs Candour nodded. "Poor Minna didn't stand a chance, living next door."

"That she didn't," agreed Bessie. "Violet soaked up every spare minute she wasn't running around after her dratted father."

"It's Mrs Renshaw's relatives we're after," said Dee, cutting into her toast and spearing a liberally cheese-coated piece. "There must be someone who should be informed."

Bessie put her head on one side, considering. "She's been off in a taxi quite a lot recently, but her visitors were mostly local. She often had people to the house, because she liked showing them around her garden. The WI speaker from last night has been a couple of times. Other than that, I can't help you. She doesn't - didn't - come in very often. Just when she wanted to bump into someone accidental-like."

"Her loss," said Dee. "If I lived over the road, I'd be in every lunchtime. This Welsh rarebit is lush."

Bessie looked pleased. "I'll tell Olive. She's my sister. It's good plain food the way we've always done it and the way Mum did it before us. I leave all the modern stuff to my Nancy up on Church Parade."

"Is that *Nancy's Fancies?* I remember her cakes from last time we were here."

"That's her. She already had the patisserie in the old dry cleaners because say what you like, folk don't come all the way down here just to buy a lemon slice, but that was only a slip of a shop. We knew there was the market for bigger, with all the new houses and the Cambridge overspill, but finding the premises was a puzzle. When the bank put up the notice about shutting, Nancy was down to Jerry Ellwood at the estate agents like a bullet. Doing very nicely now with her tacos and wraps and salads as well as the cakes. Tobias's handicrafts sell well too. It's surprising what people will buy while they're waiting for a cappuccino."

Mrs Candour chuckled. "Tell her about Violet and the puddings."

Bessie gave a broad grin. "Yes, that shows what she was like. Nancy's always done our desserts, see, ever since she was little. Up with the lark and straight down to the ovens. Lemon Meringue, Baked Alaska, Pineapple Upside-Down Cake and so on. She brings them over first thing in the morning before she opens. Well, one day, Violet sidles up to me and says in her roundabout way that she didn't suppose I'd want it generally known we buy in our cakes from a rival shop. She was after a discount off her bill, see, in return for keeping quiet. How we laughed. As if old-Fencross hasn't grown up with Nancy running in and out of the *Cosy Kettle* kitchen since she was big enough to put a pinny on. Still, it did her a favour in a way." She reached back to the counter to give Dee a business card with a colourful display of cakes on one side and '*Cakes by Nancy's Fancies, Church Parade, Fencross Parva*' on the other. "Free advertising, isn't it? A lot of visitors to the care home pop in here for a cuppa and a piece of cake, then stop off at Nancy's if they want some to take home. We wouldn't have thought of it by ourselves."

Now that was an interesting sidelight on Violet. Aloud, Dee said, "Pineapple Upside-Down Cake is my gran's favourite. That and my ma-in-law's Jamaican black rum cake were what won her over when Eithan and I first got serious. She said any fella whose mum baked like that was worth holding on to. Do you do takeaway?"

Bessie's face was wreathed in smiles. "I'll put a couple of portions in a box and add them to your bill. The old recipes are still the best."

"Thanks, that would be brilliant. Those visitors Mrs Renshaw showed around the garden - were they mostly women? No men friends at all?"

Bessie exchanged a quick glance with Mrs Candour and lowered her voice. "I wouldn't say friends, but I did see Jerry Ellwood going down her path one evening a couple of weeks ago. It was bin night, I remember, and I hadn't emptied the kitchen rubbish, so I just nipped out. I saw the light from her front door and I heard him say 'Here I am, but I can't stay long. I'm getting fish and chips' and that was it."

Interesting. Minna had mentioned Jerry Ellwood. "He's the estate agent you were talking about, yes?"

"That's right. The main shop is in Newmarket, but he's got a branch office down on New Parade next to the hairdresser. Nancy's friend Lorna works there."

She gave a bright nod and bustled off to see to another customer, leaving them to enjoy their lunch. Heroically, none of them mentioned that popping in on the way to *The Handy Plaice* in the evening was a funny time to be doing any sort of house business.

CHAPTER EIGHT

"Nobody at the café knows anything about Violet Renshaw before she came to live in Fencross Parva," reported Dee. "What they did know, they didn't much like. There might or might not be something going on with that estate agent. Oh, and she wasn't above a spot of blackmail."

"Haven't you been busy," remarked Kenelm. He couldn't really fault her. He'd done a similar thing himself by asking his mother for information.

"I don't like to waste police time, sir."

He raised a disbelieving eyebrow. "Lunch counting as work so you can submit expenses doesn't come into it, I suppose? Violet wasn't above a spot of plagiarism either. Copied out passages from one of the better known herbals and passed it off as her own knowledge according to my mama who, incidentally, was blamelessly occupied all night."

"Not much point wading through that file of pamphlet notes then," said Dee. "Suzy Emmet reckons the doctor will have next-of-kin."

"I rang the receptionist. That part of the form isn't filled in. Who did Violet blackmail?"

"Bessie at the café. It didn't work because of Violet being a newcomer and not knowing Bessie's daughter owns *Nancy's Fancies*. They all had a good laugh over that. It made me think, though. Why move here? Why come to an area where you know no one?"

"Fresh start after her husband died, one assumes."

Dee shook her head. "I got the impression from Minna that Violet had been widowed for quite some time before she moved here. Not knowing anyone is plain weird. What was she, early sixties? That's late to make new friends. You'd think she'd need *someone*."

Kenelm frowned. "Expound."

"Memories. Human nature. Think of Calli Nelson - she relocated from London, but Fencross was where her uncle lived and where she'd spent holidays. Eithan's gran and her sister came here from Jamaica because the UK wanted nurses, but they were *young*, not even twenty, and they had each other. Older people don't usually move to a completely new area unless it's for a job or to be near family. If my mum ever left my dad - which she won't however much I tell her to - she'd want to go somewhere familiar, somewhere near her support group."

Kenelm stared at his constable without seeing her. She was right. He'd come back to Fencross Parva when life had fallen apart, despite saying years ago when he left home that he was out of here for good. He'd held out against returning to the Manor, but that was about it. "Sound reasoning. Irrelevant unless the post-mortem comes back with anything suspicious, but sound nevertheless."

"Thank you, sir. Another question. Why are we not going through Violet's handbag to find her personal info?"

This time his stare was exasperated and directed mostly at himself. What was happening to him? How had he forgotten all women kept their life in their bag? The number of times he'd seen Sarah transferring everything from one shoulder bag to the next, even crumpled tissues and stubs of pencils. "Because I'm not female, dammit.

Nor is the chief. Blame the inequality in the hierarchy. There was a handbag in the bedside cupboard. Take a photo first, then list everything."

Maybe Dee wouldn't defect to plain clothes, he thought as she bounced away to get it. Maybe she'd leapfrog straight to Chief Constable. He only hoped her husband would continue to work in the MOT garage and service his car. With the hit his finances had been taking recently, he couldn't afford to buy a new one.

Dee went through Violet Renshaw's handbag with increasing mystification. Very little cash in the purse. A screen-locked mobile phone with no emergency contact showing. No photos, driving licence or passport. A neat packet of folded tissues, some scrunched-up sweet wrappers, but no old supermarket receipts or scribbled phone numbers or minicab cards. It wasn't natural. Did she tidy it every day? There *was* a diary, supermarket loyalty card, credit card and bank card. There was also a fat notebook with closely-written random annoyances in it. Dee made out *'bank clerk rude'*, *'newspaper damp on step'* and *'Rhona Lee bought last Flower Arranger'* before giving up.

Finally, in a hidden zipped flap, there was a thin notebook with dates and facts. It looked like some sort of account book. The first entry was dated six years previously and simply said *Minna £2*. The next line was a few days after that and said *Minna £1*. Dee assumed she'd lent her neighbour a couple of pounds here and there and recorded it so as not to forget, but then the next entry said *6am Nancy's Fancies to Cosy Kettle*.

"Wait a minute," said Dee aloud. She skimmed the rest of the page. *10pm Margaret Dearlove on common in nightgown. JE 27 mins. Minna £2. 5am NF to CK. JE 44 mins. 11am Desmond Saxon to dustbin with bottles* . She turned the page in growing disgust.

"Found something?" asked the guvnor, looking up.

"Violet spied on her neighbours and wrote it all down. What a cow."

"Show me."

Dee passed over the notebook. "She started as soon as she moved in. The dates tally with the first ones for the household bills. The entries for the *Cosy Kettle* are what she used to try her spot of blackmail."

"How to make friends and influence people. What's your reading of the petty cash to Minna Saxon?"

"Times she lent her money."

"I don't know," said the guvnor thoughtfully. "My mother says it's common knowledge that Minna has kleptomaniac tendencies. Most people discreetly gloss over it."

"There is that little bowl of loose change on the hall shelf," said Dee. "That could be awfully tempting. Minna probably kids herself she's only borrowing it. But why wouldn't Violet have kept it out of sight once she realised?"

"Power? The knowledge she had a hold on her neighbour? Annie says she wasn't a nice woman. I suppose there's nothing in the handbag regarding any relatives?"

"Not unless she's written it in the larger book there, which is a right mess."

Dee watched the guvnor skim through the notebook, his fastidious face expressing distaste. "Stream of consciousness stuff. Everything written down as she thinks of it. Comments on the newspaper being torn all mixed up with next door shouting at her and not being able to buy a custard tart in *Nancy's Fancies*. She seems to have been a very discontented individual. Put it by for later and try the desk drawers."

"With particular reference to official documents?"

"Indeed. Will forms, solicitor's correspondence, address books, anything over six years old..."

Dee pulled open the top drawer. Underneath neatly arranged pens, pencils, notepaper and envelopes, was an A4 envelope with WILL written on it. Even as she pulled it out, she was thinking it was a pretty weird place to keep an important document. She carefully extracted the two sheets inside. By the time she'd read to the end she was feeling even less charitable towards the late Violet. "I thought this might be the will, but it isn't. What a foul woman."

The guvnor's phone pinged. "What do you mean?" he said, thumbing the screen to read the text that had come in.

"It looks as if Violet was playing a really nasty game."

She heard him draw a breath as he read his text. When he spoke, his voice was remote. "Why?"

She flicked the page with disgust. "Because this leaves everything to *'my great friend Minna Alexandra Saxon'*. Except she hasn't signed it. How much do you bet it was a con to keep Minna sweet?"

Dee expected him to exhibit a similar scepticism. Instead, there was a troubled calculation in his eyes. "Well, that's fun, isn't it? Would you like to know what this text says?"

"If you want to tell me, sir," she said cautiously.

"It's from the chief. We are to hold ourselves in readiness for a communication from Detective Superintendent Macready. Violet Renshaw was poisoned."

I knew it, thought Dee, followed by the realisation that the draft will was a hell of a motive if Minna was as hard-up as she appeared to be. She cleared her throat. "So, what do we do now?"

He raised that eyebrow again. "Keep looking until we're told otherwise. Find someone to inform. Once the crime scene guys get here, we aren't going to have another chance."

Why did that matter? Dislike of leaving a job half done? Family! That argument between Violet and his mother. He wanted advance warning of anything that might be turned up in a more thorough search. Dee put on her best following-orders voice and said, "Right you are, sir. I wonder if there's anything in those two notebooks? If she wrote down details about people she had grudges against, as well as those she knew secrets about, she might also mention where the real will was."

He looked at her for such a long moment she feared she'd overstepped the mark. "Your point?"

"Just that it might save a search. Terrible tiny writing though. We could step over to Calli's and borrow her scanner. It's got one of those enlarging options."

Another long look. "Good notion. I'll do that now. You carry on here. Any sort of result would be nice."

There were no other documents in the drawer. To Dee's mind, that was proof Minna had been supposed to see the fake will, to keep her devoted. The other drawer yielded the parish magazine, a list of useful local contacts, the WI schedule for the year, ditto the gardening club and her Christmas card list. All innocuous.

"Christmas cards!" she exclaimed aloud. "Of course!"

Annie took the short cut back from the rectory via Forge Lane. In days gone by, the lane would have been busy with horses being taken to be shod, or carts waiting for axles to be mended or wheels to be re-spoked. Now the smithy was the Old Forge restaurant, but the track alongside still ran down to connect with the footpath and bridleway between Mulberry Lane and Much Clattering. As her feet took the familiar route, Annie's head was a rush of thoughts: things needing to be done for tonight's loathsome visitors, her current painting and when she was going to get it finished, secret whispering hopes about whether Heather Meadows would really be in touch and how much she'd be likely to pay, ideas for the big painting Bunty wanted for her living room wall, the tiny loneliness of seeing Calli and Gideon together, an odd conundrum Rev Robin had unwittingly planted in her brain - and the ever-present background despair of Mum slipping in and out of reality.

Robin had understood the despair. Annie hadn't expected that. She didn't think it had come from pastoral training either. Just a quiet 'my grandad went last year and I have never hated an illness more' and a brief squeeze of the hand, then she was listening as Annie mumbled that it was early onset dementia and it wasn't fair. Mum had been so vital, so full of life. People would go into the dry cleaning shop just to talk to her, to be cheered by her flashing smile and tumbling laugh. Now there were days when she could barely remember who her own daughter was.

"Life isn't fair," said Robin. She wrote Mum's name down carefully and asked if there was anything she could chat to her about that might strike a chord.

"Gardens, plants, dogs, musical theatre. Aunty Dora used to be on the stage and would give us an impromptu show when she visited. Only if Grandma was at work, though. Grandma didn't believe in enjoying yourself."

Annie hadn't intended to stay at the rectory for lunch, but they'd been hanging Robin's painting and talking about Mum, and when they came out of the study, Bunty was looking through Gideon's designs.

"Gifted chap, isn't he? He knows someone who can do the upholstery. Which of these couches do you fancy, Robin? And after seeing your painting, what I'd really like is something big and full of light to go on the wall in here. Not a talking point, but something to tie the whole room together. What do you suggest, Annie? Have you ever tackled a really large canvas? I'd pay the going rate, of course."

Before Annie knew it, she was taking dimensions and scrolling through the portfolio on her phone to give Bunty some ideas and eating crusty bread and fancy cheese. She'd even had the scary, fluttery feeling that comes from knowing how the painting should go and being terrified she couldn't do it. It had been lovely, just like being a full-time artist *should* be.

But now it was real life again and she was late with the visitor preparations. Coming down to earth hurt as much as ever. She reached the end of the footpath and looked along Mulberry Lane before crossing the road. The police car was still outside Riverdene. Kenelm was striding towards her.

"If you want to ask questions, you'll have to do it on the move," she warned. "I'm in a hurry."

"As am I. Macready's on his way and Dee's searching for anything remotely like relatives or legal people, to which end I need Calli to enlarge a couple of notebooks."

"If it's notes for Violet's pamphlets, I shouldn't bother. Most of her text is erroneous and the rest is copied."

"So my mother informs me, in confirmation of which she advanced the opinion that if Violet was dead, she'd probably been trying out her own remedies. Prophetic woman, my mother."

Annie gave a snort of laughter. "I can't imagine her being that stupid, sadly. Do as I say, not as I do, that was Violet. Lovely thought though." She opened her gate.

"Are you all right?" asked Kenelm. "You seem distracted."

"I am. I stayed to lunch at the rectory and now I'm

late making beds and vacuuming carpets." *God, listen to me. How has my life gone this wrong? Quick, talk about something else so he doesn't think I'm whining.* "Robin said something odd. We were talking about Mum and Aunty Dora, and she asked how it was that Grandma was so joyless when she had two such lively, fun daughters? And I didn't know. She was just Grandma. Grim, stern, always busy, thrifty to the nth degree, closed in."

A thoughtful look crossed Kenelm's face. "Grim yes, I remember that, but she was a handsome woman. What was your grandfather like?"

Handsome? Annie supposed she had been. "I don't know. He died long before I was born. That's why she went back to work. He only left a tiny pension and she had the house to keep up and two young children to look after. She was a solicitor's secretary in Ely. Mum and Aunty Dora had to get their own tea when they came home from school because Grandma's bus didn't get back until six o'clock. Wouldn't be allowed these days, would it?"

"Social services would be up in arms. Maybe that was it? She didn't have time for fun, so forgot how to have it."

His words had the clean sword-slice of truth. Annie stared at him in the silence they brought. "That's really depressing."

He looked as stricken as she felt. "Isn't it. What a thought to take back to work. Sorry. See you later."

She hurried indoors, then forced herself to slow down, reflecting uneasily that she was in danger of turning into Grandma herself if she wasn't careful. It wasn't until she was battling the second guest-room duvet into its cover that Kenelm's earlier words sunk in. *Prophetic woman, my mother.* Did he mean Violet had been poisoned? But how? When? She'd been fine yesterday evening. Eating, arguing, everything had been completely as usual. How could she possibly have been poisoned?

CHAPTER NINE

"I think," said Kenelm, who was gazing out of the window while Calli photocopied and enlarged the notebooks he'd brought over, "that I probably wasn't sympathetic enough when Lydia walked out on you, Gideon."

Calli exchanged a quick glance with Gideon and continued to scan and print. She was also saving the scans to file, but considerately wasn't mentioning the fact in case Kenelm thought it his duty to object.

"You're twenty years late, but apology accepted. What's brought this on?"

Kenelm was still staring out at the High Street. "My brain doesn't seem to be functioning properly. Not only did I accidentally let on to Annie that Violet was poisoned, Dee had to remind me earlier that the first place to look for a woman's contacts is in her handbag."

Calli suppressed an amused snort.

"Delayed reaction," said Gideon. "Tell me more about the poison."

Kenelm spun around, dismay on his face. "Christ, now I've told you! Do me a favour and pretend to forget it, okay? All I know is coniine with a double-i, whatever that may be. The case has been allocated to Superintendent Macready so the chance of me finding out any more is minimal. Any sort of poison means forensics and a specialist search squad. I doubt he'll need my local knowledge."

"Ahem, whose local knowledge?"

Kenelm threw him a sarcastic look. "As I recall, we pooled resources last time. Why are you here, anyway? Don't you have work to do?"

"Client cancelled."

Calli's phone rang. She stopped listening to the men and answered it.

"I'm testing a theory," said Dee's voice. "Who is on your Christmas card list?"

Calli groaned. "Oh God, everyone! It takes me days to write them all. Friends of Mum and Dad who have known me forever, people from all the libraries where I've ever worked, friends from college. Friends of David's who still politely send a card so I have to send one back. The only two school friends apart from Meriel that I've kept in touch with. It goes on and on. Why?"

"That's what I thought. Is the guvnor there?"

"Yes, hold on, I'll pass you over."

"Don't bother, just tell him Violet's Christmas card list doesn't contain anyone who isn't local. No one from more than six years ago."

Calli's mouth fell open. "What?" she said incredulously. "That's not possible. It's what Christmas cards are *for*, keeping up with people once a year."

"Not natural, is it? You'll probably need to explain the significance, bless him."

She ended the call. Calli scanned the final page and handed the notebooks back to Kenelm while she gave him Dee's message.

"Christmas card list?" he said with the wariness of a man who for eighteen years had simply scrawled his name on the cards his wife put in front of him.

Calli hid a grin. Dee had been right. "They're a roll-call of our lives," she explained. "Politeness, obligations and assuaging of guilt all in one annual fell swoop. My list goes back thirty years."

Kenelm frowned. "You're implying Violet Renshaw amputated her past when she moved to Fencross Parva."

Calli nodded. "Has to be."

"In hiding, I wonder?" mused Kenelm. "Escaping from someone? That'll interest Macready. He'll put the police computer into meltdown looking for a trail."

"Can't be that difficult. The bank would know where she used to live. Don't they keep everything?" Calli remembered something else. "Her husband's death certificate will have their residence at the time."

"Or try the solicitor she engaged when buying the bungalow," suggested Gideon. "They have to have a record of her last address."

Kenelm made a tetchy noise. "You think I'm an amateur? I've already left messages. Thanks for the enlargements. I suppose you haven't got an envelope I can put them in?"

"No problem," said Calli, getting one out of a drawer. "See you later."

After he'd gone, Gideon met her eyes. "What sort of poison did he say?"

Calli read her hasty scrawl. "Coniine. I've never heard of it."

"I'll look it up and make a fresh pot of tea. You start reading through Violet's notebook. If we're going to solve this before Kenelm's senior investigating officer takes him off the case, we can't waste any time."

Kenelm was thinking exactly the same thing. Irritatingly, he'd only just returned to Riverdene, put the two notebooks with the rest of Violet's stuff and verified the truth about the Christmas card list when he heard the sound of car doors slamming.

"Nice of them to signal their arrival," he said sourly.

"They don't call him Speedy Macready for nothing, sir," replied Dee. "He's probably on his way somewhere else and thought he'd drop by to see the lie of the land. Shall I let him in?"

"It'll be better for your promotion prospects than leaving him on the doorstep."

The next hour took the form of a brisk walk-through of the bungalow, the summoning of a very flustered Minna Saxon to repeat her story about finding Violet and the arrival of the forensics team.

"I'll leave you to see they've got everything necessary, Inspector," said Macready by way of farewell. "Case consultation nine am tomorrow at the station and I'll want a full report before you finish tonight. Keep trying the solicitor. People don't simply appear out of thin air. If she's cut her ties as thoroughly as you are conjecturing, there will be a reason."

In other words, stick to the routine enquiries like a good little uniform. "Yes, sir. What about the church hall where she spent time yesterday evening?"

Macready regarded him with intense dislike. "Seal it to await forensics. The team can continue over there once they finish here. Inform the vicar and impound the keys."

"Just like that," muttered Kenelm as the cars pulled away. From the bedroom came the sound of forensic murmurs. Already there had been pointed looks from the specialist search crew regarding his continued presence in the bungalow. Kenelm glanced at his watch. "It's time you were away, Dee. I'll see you at the station in the morning."

"Yes, sir. Or I could come and pick you up? Odds-on we'll be back here after the briefing. Seems a shame to use your own petrol when the squad car has a full tank."

Now what was she up to? "You have some pressing reason for wanting to leave home forty minutes early in order to chauffeur me?"

"Overtime, sir. Video games cost money. Also it's a school morning and Eithan is way better than I am at getting the little tykes up, dressed and breakfasted."

He waved a hand. "Consider it authorised. Buzz me when you're five minutes away."

He made one further attempt to ring the solicitor, who had certainly gone home for the day by now, left another message, sent another email and told the forensic team he was going home to work on his report and to contact him if they needed anything.

"There's nothing in any of the waste bins or the recycling bins," said one of the search team accusingly.

"It was refuse collection today. They come around at six in the morning."

"They shouldn't have been allowed to take the bins."

Kenelm's eyes narrowed. "I repeat, *sergeant*, the domestic waste and recycling lorries come at six in the morning. I did not get the call apprising me of a fatality and instructing me to investigate until 07:23. I beg your pardon, did you say something?"

"No, sir. I'll be getting on, sir."

"You do that." Kenelm left for the church hall, the rectory and then home, taking his notes and enlargements with him. After that display of insubordination, the search team could make their own damn copies.

In the back garden, Annie was shooing the hens into coops for the night. She looked at him grumpily. "If you're after the microwave, tonight's visitors have taken over the kitchen already."

"Gideon and Calli invited me for a meal."

"Lucky you."

"I'll go in via the front so I can get changed without

you being asked why you have police in the house." As he spoke, he was conscious of mild resentment. If he hadn't been so unsettled about the case, he'd have laughed in disbelief that he was so at home here now as to habitually use the back door as all old-Fencross folk did. Gideon would be amused at the irony.

He'd turned to go when Annie said abruptly, "Was Violet really poisoned?"

It would be common knowledge soon enough. "So I'm told."

"What sort?"

"Coniine, apparently. I haven't had a chance to look it up yet."

She turned pale. "Coniine? That comes from hemlock."

He stared. "What, like Socrates? And Keats writing *'as though of hemlock I had drunk'*? Annie, that's archaic."

"You going to tell it or shall I? It doesn't stop it being toxic. According to the herbals, hemlock causes a creeping paralysis starting from the toes and working up. It's one of the things to look out for when foraging."

"In what way?"

"I mean just touching it can affect some people. It can be mistaken for parsley, except I think the stem has purple spots. I'll have to check. Other names for it are Fool's Parsley and Poison Parsley. Violet must have picked some by mistake. I wouldn't put it past her. I'll have to search the common."

"Why on earth?"

"In case that's where she found it, of course," said Annie impatiently. "She's often on the common, creeping around to see what Dinah and I have come across that we are meanly keeping secret from the wider world. That's how she found the orchid. Hemlock is really poisonous, Kenelm. Humans and livestock, both. It'll need digging out and burning."

Kenelm put a hand on her arm to restrain her. "Wait. We don't know she picked it herself. If she did, we don't know where. I suppose her notebook might mention it."

She shook him off. "I can't run the risk."

"Why you?"

"You see anyone else doing it?"

This was one stubborn woman. Kenelm took a deep breath. "It's starting to get dark. The common is large. We don't know for sure how the coniine was ingested. Wait until I get the full report. I'll ask for it as a priority and say it's a matter of public safety. That's within my remit, even if nothing else is. If they find hemlock leaves in her gut as opposed to, I don't know, powder or juice, we can have the common searched. That way the police will do it rather than you. You can run us off some nice clear identification pictures." Then, as she still looked mutinous he added, "It can't be widespread or there would be more casualties. Look, come to supper at Calli's. If it concerns Fencross, Gideon will want to know. Talk it over with him."

She glowered, but he sensed her relenting. "I haven't been asked."

"Annie, you've been friends with Gideon for forty years. Invitations matter?"

CHAPTER TEN

"This is a really sick notebook," said Calli, taking a break from reading the screen to pick up the mug Gideon put in front of her. "They both are."

"In what way?" said Gideon. "I've looked up hemlock. Its appearance is similar to wild carrot and wild parsnip when it's tall, and it is often mistaken for parsley when it's young."

"Crikey. Why aren't all foragers dead then?"

"Purple spots on the stalk and a nasty smell, apparently."

"Lovely. Anyway, Violet's fat notebook records every single time someone annoyed her and what they did. You wouldn't believe the pettiness. The thin one has got potentially damaging observations and dates. It also has sinister little ticks against people's names."

"Do the ticks in the thin book match up with the grudges in the fat book?"

"Quick, aren't you? I thought of that. They might do, yes. The ticks are dated, but the grudges aren't. A number of the same names crop up in both places. Who is Luke Roberts?"

"One of Greta and Sean's brood. Limb of Satan when he was younger. He delivers the papers and used to sing in the choir before his voice broke. Reverend Silver had a touching faith in the power of the church to turn kids to the light. His dad works for Ed Gray at Home Farm. He must be sixteen or seventeen now. Why?"

"There's a tick against his name soon after Violet moved here."

"How would she have known a scruffy kid?"

"That's why I'm asking you," said Calli patiently. "Does he have a name for mugging old ladies or revving up scooters on quiet residential roads?"

"Not six years ago, no. The most he could have done in those days was crash into her on his bike on the way to school because he'd been late finishing his paper round."

Something clicked in Calli's memory. "Did he deliver to Mulberry Lane? There was something near the start of the fat book about the newspaper being late."

"Probably. He's had the paper round concession on the whole village for years. But, Calli, people don't hold grudges about papers being late."

"Violet held grudges about everything. I've never known anyone as touchy as she seemed to be." Calli scrolled back through the scans. "Here, see? And later on she says the paper arrived ripped."

Gideon peered over her shoulder. "So she did." Then, in an altered voice. "What's the date for when his name was ticked?"

Calli obligingly brought up the image of the other book. "There you are. Does it mean something to you?"

Gideon tapped the date into his phone. "Not as such, but it was a Sunday."

"Is that significant?"

"It could be. Remember what Annie said about how the belladonna club got its name?"

Calli stared at him. "You think this might be the Sunday the gardening club did the arrangement of deadly nightshade berries above the choir stalls? Surely that was accidental."

"Luke's name is ticked. It's a possibility and if so, it was deliberate. I agree it seems petty just to get even for a late newspaper. Anyone might have touched them. Any of the kids might have eaten them for a dare. What sort of a monster would do that?"

A wriggle of horror slid through Calli. "An unbalanced one. If it was on purpose, Violet could have done other nasty stuff to repay people who had offended her. It might give someone a motive for poisoning her. We should tell Kenelm."

"For sure. Let's go through more entries and present him with a list."

"If I've got the stomach for it," muttered Calli.

By the time Kenelm and Annie arrived that evening, they had amassed a casserole, a bottle of wine and seventeen instances of ticked names matching up with previous grudges. There were lots more, but they'd both decided they needed a break. Awkwardly, three of the ticks were against Annie's name.

"No, that can't be right," said Annie. "I've annoyed Violet way more than three times. What did she do to revenge herself on me?"

"She doesn't say. She's dated the ticks, though. That might help you work it out." Gideon pushed the pages they'd printed across the table.

"You know," mused Kenelm. "I could have sworn you only made the one set of enlargements."

Gideon looked at him blandly. "What good is local knowledge if the puzzle is locked away in the evidence box?"

"Point."

Annie frowned at the list. "The first one is a long time ago. The original grudge must have been when I had the row with her at the gardening club talk."

"Figures," said Calli. "She mentions you insulted her."

"I only told the truth. I wonder how she repaid me?"

"Got the public health inspectors in? Shopped you to the Inland Revenue?"

"Should I be listening to this?" asked Kenelm.

Annie shook her head. "My business is all above board, but I wasn't doing Airbnb then anyway. Mum was still at home, so I didn't need to find the money for residential care. Just as well. I had my hands full simply with..." She trailed off, horrified comprehension on her face.

"With what?" asked Kenelm.

"With stopping her wandering on to the common at all hours of the day and night. You remember, Gideon, the gate used to have a simple latch until you put the bolts on. I assumed Mum was opening it herself on her midnight rambles, even though she'd promised she wouldn't. Suppose it had been unlatched and left open so she just drifted through? It would be easy for Violet to sneak around the edge of the common and do it, and I know for sure she reported Mum to the police 'in a terribly worried voice' a couple of times. The caller was always anonymous, but Luke Roberts overheard her in the phone box once and let me know. I didn't enquire what a kid of his age was doing hanging around phone boxes that late at night."

"The cow. That's really mean," said Calli, indignant on Annie's behalf.

Annie turned in the general direction of the care home. "Sorry, Mum. Maybe you weren't to blame after all."

"What about the other ticks against your name?" said Gideon. "They're well after I put the bolts on the gate."

"Where? Oh, I see. Four years ago?" Annie scratched her head. "That might be the VAT inspection. There was a rash of them. I had one for my artwork business, so did *Nancy's Fancies*, so did the riding stables."

"Oh good," said Calli. "I mean, not good, obviously, but there was something about the girl from the stables laughing at her when she complained about the horses using the road outside her house as a lavatory. What's her name? I can mark that off as matched too."

Gideon regarded her with astonishment. "Violet complained about the horses? Why did she buy a house in a country village, then? You'd have thought she'd rush out and shovel up the manure for her roses. That's what Great-grandad used to do."

Kenelm stirred. "Dee mentioned it was a strange choice of location when she didn't know anyone in the area. I wondered if she moved here because she was hiding."

"And was resentful about having to move?" said Calli. "We did notice there was a long gap with no ticks at all. Maybe she settled down and then something wound her up again."

Kenelm studied the enlargement and smiled suddenly. "The gap is over lockdown. She wouldn't have had the opportunity to do mischief."

"Lockdown!" Gideon met Calli's eyes, reflecting her own amazement at not having thought of that. "I'd completely forgotten. At the time, I couldn't see how it would ever end."

A nostalgic sigh escaped Kenelm. "It was lovely. Crime rate went right down. I got to go home on time after every shift. Spent longer with the boys. Got all my paperwork backlogs cleared..."

"Lucky you," said Gideon. "I had to fix my own roof because the entire building trade was furloughed."

"I believe that was spun as adding to one's personal skill set," said Kenelm. He tapped the list. "The thing is, if all these little revenges were directed at one person it would be harassment. Spread out over six years and so many people, they're irritations. Unless Dee is right and Violet went in for blackmail too. Judging by her bank statements, she spent way over her income. She didn't stint on her shopping, took taxis everywhere and her bank balance has gone down steadily since she moved in. She might easily have wanted to top up her day-to-day cash. Any thoughts on your third tick, Annie? It's just over a year ago."

Annie's eyes travelled down the list. "Oh," she said in a flat voice. "That would be about the time the postcard came for Mum, the one supposedly from Oscar."

"Oscar?" asked Calli. Too late she saw Gideon's warning shake of the head.

Annie glanced up, her eyes desolate. "Oscar was the bastard who charmed Mum into thinking he loved her, then broke her heart by leaving without a word. It was years ago now, but she's never forgotten him no matter what else she struggles to remember. That postcard was what tipped her over the edge. It wasn't from Oscar, obviously, he'd been long gone. I knew it was a fake. I told Mum it was a fake. Now I know who sent it. Violet was a dab hand at soaking up gossip." She swallowed. "Irritations, did you call them, Kenelm? That wasn't an irritation. That was deliberate malevolence. If I'd known for sure Violet had sent it…" She broke off. "It's probably a good thing she's already dead."

Calli stretched across the table and squeezed her hand.

"Christ, Annie, don't say that sort of thing to a copper. Have you no sense of self-preservation? Definitely don't say it to Macready if he asks."

"I said *if* I'd known, but I didn't. Besides, you're off duty."

"He's never off duty," replied Gideon. "He's blue and silver right through. He won't report this conversation, but everything we say is seeping into his soul. He wants to get to the bottom of Violet's death as much as we do."

Kenelm nodded. "I'd rather know the worst straight away. Forewarned is forearmed. If the death wasn't accidental, Macready is going to find plenty of suspects as soon as he starts analysing the notebooks. He won't like that. He'll go for the obvious person first, the one with knowledge and opportunity."

"Damn," said Gideon. "If he questions her, Annie isn't going to be able to prevaricate now she knows the dates."

"*And* she's known to hate the victim *and* her boot prints are all over Violet's flowerbed *and* she has poisonous-plant knowledge," agreed Kenelm.

"I am here, you know," said Annie.

Calli made a sympathetic face at her. "They do this when they get talking. All the not-liking-each-other is pure fabrication."

Gideon drummed his fingers on the table. "Force the issue, then. Get the whole village talking about Violet."

"Putting everybody on their guard?" said Kenelm, askance. "Thanks very much."

"No, just make it common currency that she wasn't liked. Then when your detectives start interviewing people, they'll receive the same impression from everyone, that she was a bit of a nuisance in a low-grade way."

A meditative look crossed Kenelm's face. "So Macready can't ignore it and is forced to widen his scope rather than concentrate on Annie, you mean? Yes, that could work."

Calli regarded them both affectionately. "But you still want to find out what petty revenges she took for all the annoyances, don't you?"

"Yes, I do," said Gideon. "Let's start with the most recent and work back."

"I wasn't living here, so it's no use me looking at dates," said Calli, "but if you give me names, I can go through the first list to match them with the grievances. We've got half an hour before the food's ready. See how far we can get."

CHAPTER ELEVEN

Annie sat back, the conversation muted by the pounding of her thoughts. Violet. Violet Renshaw had been the one who sent that cruel postcard to Mum. Annie had suspected it at the time. If she shut her eyes, she could still see it.

Wish you were here but it's a good thing you're not because I've got a rich young girlfriend now and she gets jealous when I kiss other women. That's life, eh? Hope you are well. Oscar x

Annie had ripped the postcard to pieces in a fury and thrown the whole thing away, and Mum had spent the next month turning the house upside down searching for it. Every time they'd gone out she would ask people if they'd seen Oscar, if they knew where he was, no matter that he'd left Fencross Parva a dozen years before. And Violet had been full of sugary sympathy and had tittered about 'poor Mrs Dearlove' behind her back. And then she'd look soulful and pretend to catch herself and say she knew she wasn't really a Mrs, but it seemed more respectable to call her that, didn't it?

The memory brought bile to Annie's throat. She was overcome with such a rush of hatred for the dead woman she didn't hear Gideon asking her a question.

"Earth to Annie. The lady with the Afghan hound. What was the story about that?"

Annie forced herself to concentrate. "Pat Williams? The RSPCA swooped on her because they'd had a report she was mistreating her dog. As if. She might argue with everyone at the drop of a hat, but she dotes on Rupert. The informant claimed she tied him up for hours and left him all alone."

"Does she?"

"No, of course not. Rupert goes everywhere with her, even in the car. She straps him into the passenger seat and anyone else she gives a lift has to cram in the back."

"Aha," said Calli. "Violet mentioned that. She was not impressed. So that's another matching tick."

"What happened with the RSPCA?" asked Gideon.

"Nothing. They apologised and said they get no end of false calls."

"I don't suppose they logged the caller?"

"Probably, but they wouldn't give out the information. Maybe if they got a lot of calls from the same number, they'd flag it and report it."

Kenelm made a note. "It's something to look into. Another irritation, which fits with her modus operandi. How many instances have you matched?"

Gideon looked at Calli's list. "Quite a lot." He hesitated. "There's one here for your mother. July 16th last year."

Annie gave a short laugh. "16th July was the village show. I know what that will be. Violet won the single long-stemmed rose category. Somebody had slit the stem of Dinah's *Velvet Fragrance* so it wilted. Plenty of people had their suspicions but no one had seen anything."

"Had she been expected to win?"

She looked at him in disbelief. "Kenelm, this is your mother. Of course she was expected to win. She wiped the floor with the other rose categories. A similar thing happened with Rhona Lee's runner beans. Ten perfectly matched beans, and someone had run a sharp knife diagonally across them. The entry had to be disqualified. Rhona was furious."

"Rhona?" Calli riffled through the pages. "There is a mention of Rhona buying the last issue of the *Flower Arranger* in the shop. It was years before, though."

"Lockdown," Annie reminded her. "Village show was cancelled twice."

"You're right. Here's the tick. Violet must have waited her chance. Fancy having that much bitterness inside. How much of this are you going to pass on to Mr Macready, Kenelm?"

Kenelm's words came quite slowly. "Strictly speaking, it's not my job. He doesn't know I have the enlargements. He doesn't like amateur sleuths. He doesn't consider me part of the detecting team. I'm an intelligent mule, employed to organise personnel and kit and to mop up the actions no one else is doing."

"That wasn't the question."

"I know. I'm thinking it through. If his team figure all this out, that's fine. If I mention it, he'll remember my connection to the village and wonder who I'm trying to shield. I'd rather have evidence of something more than a mess of petty annoyances before I lay any information before him."

Annie met his eyes, feeling her way around what she wanted to say. "That makes sense. The thing is, if I'd known for certain this time last year that Violet sent the postcard, I might have been tempted to take action. I could easily have trashed her garden or taken an axe to her horrible fence until I felt better. All these months later, I'd settle for complete exposure."

Kenelm nodded. "You're saying the passage of time cools everything down? I agree. And I take Gideon's point about somehow letting it be known there was a widespread feeling against her. I do think we need a list of people, what small grievance she had against them, how she got back at them, dates for both if possible. I won't volunteer it unless I'm asked or unless it becomes so pertinent that I can't withhold it, but when I do, it will be the full thing. My feeling is that the whole package dilutes the importance of the individual aggravations."

"You mean expanding the list of suspects and at the same time contracting it to someone whose capacity for holding grudges matched her own?" said Calli.

"Something like that, yes."

Annie said nothing. She had been visited by the most horrifying realisation. Violet had sent that postcard to get even with *her*, not with Mum. So Mum's dementia was her fault. Grandma always said a bad temper reaps a worse reward. She'd said Annie should learn to govern hers. She'd been right. Again.

"I'll type it all up tomorrow," promised Calli. "For now, let's clear this away, top up the wine glasses and eat. Annie, you want to cut us up some bread to have with it?"

"Sure," said Annie, glad to be busy, glad to be in Calli's bright kitchen with friends and conversation and a meal to share, glad to push away those rushing, swamping, guilt-laden dark thoughts for as long as she possibly could.

Friday morning. The autopsy report was in. Small fragments of hemlock leaf had been found in Violet Renshaw's digestive system along with salad, quiche, cake and wine. That made it a case. As far as Detective Superintendent Macready was concerned, with budget and manpower cuts making every day a balance of unpalatable decisions, he would like it to be a case of accidental death caused by the victim herself. All done and dusted inside twenty-four hours.

This much was clear to Kenelm within three minutes

of the case meeting starting. It was equally clear why he was being retained. Macready didn't like him, but he appreciated his efficiency. With Kenelm managing the groundwork, Macready could deploy his plain clothes men somewhere more useful until the basics had been completed.

The superintendent regarded him now down the full length of the table. "To summarise, the deceased was an amateur botanist whose facts were frequently inaccurate. She could have picked hemlock thinking it was parsley, and sprinkled it on her quiche, muddling her senses with some very posh plonk. That's one scenario. Additionally, she had been to a talk that evening, during which various foraged dishes were served to the company at large. There are more possibilities for accident there. I want the speaker contacted and everyone at that meeting asked if they were ill, or if they saw what the deceased ate or drank." He gave a sardonic smile. "The suggestion has been made that hemlock may be growing on the common ground backing on to Mrs Renshaw's property. This is sheer genius. It enables me to recharge the funds for a search against the public health purse. Visible police presence at no cost to the department. You can have half-a-dozen PCs including Bryce to see to the search and the questioning, Gray. How you use them is your business, but you only get them for one shift because some antisocial thug has torched the leisure centre and they'll be needed to patrol the streets here later on to deter copycats. List of questions to ask are in your actions now. I'll review the next stage once I have your results. Off you go."

In other words, Macready knew everyone hated long, fruitless searches and was therefore putting him in charge of a long, fruitless search of the common, with a side order of checking the health of everyone who had been at the WI meeting. No one would have guessed from Kenelm's regulation nod of the head and noncommittal assent that this was exactly the outcome he had been hoping for.

"You called it," he said to Dee when he came out. "Back to Fencross Parva to comb the common for hemlock plants with whoever hasn't already been nabbed to clear up the leisure centre."

"That'll be fun, sir."

"Not for you it won't. You get to walk the streets with Phyllis Winterbottom's list of WI attendees and ask if anyone at the meeting had ill-effects after sampling the food."

Dee glanced at the lowering sky. "I suppose I can't sit in Calli's nice dry library and phone them?"

"Correct. Door-to-door is all about body language. But you can sit in Calli's nice dry library to enter your reports when you're done. I'll find you there."

As it happened, it wasn't Phyllis Winterbottom who had the list, it was Julie Bamber who lived further down the High Street. "If it had been last year, I could have helped you," said Phyllis with a gracious smile, "but this year I'm the chair and Julie is the secretary, so she will have the record of attendance."

And God forbid any jobs should accidentally overlap. "Thank you," said Dee. "Can you remember what you ate at the meeting yourself? Did you experience any discomfort?"

"A piece of coffee-and-walnut cake made by Bonita Ellwood and a cup of tea. Delicious. No ill effects at all."

Oh good. Cakes too. Add them to the list, Dee. "Thank you." She pretended to check her notes. "You didn't taste the samples from the talk?"

Phyllis Winterbottom looked serenely sorrowful. "I'm afraid I was far too busy."

Julie Bamber was a cheerful, untidy soul with three small grandchildren underfoot. She nevertheless gave the impression of being a lot more efficient than her chairperson.

"List of attendees? Yes, I can run you one off if Phyllis says it's okay. Data protection and privacy, you know. Shocking thing about Violet, not that I liked her. I'm not sure many did, to be honest."

"Several people have said that," replied Dee. "Was it her manner?"

"Always knew best. Wanted to be top dog. Chloe, just because I'm talking, it doesn't mean you can draw on the wall. Use your drawing pad." She turned back to Dee. "Sorry, I look after them twice a week while my daughter works." She nodded at her granddaughter, now scribbling on a page of her sketch book. "Violet was like madam, here. Always needed to know you were paying attention to her. I slapped her down once at a WI meeting and if looks could kill I'd have been pushing up the daisies right there and then."

"Oh dear. What was that about?"

"Blowed if I can remember. It might have been when I was treasurer and she 'couldn't help seeing there was no entry for insurance on the annual accounts'. I pointed out that if she read the notes, I'd explained it had fallen at the end of the previous year so had come out twice then. And of course everyone groaned and told her to drop it because they remembered the fuss that was made at the time and didn't want to waste another ten minutes going over old ground. I tell you, I could *feel* her seething."

As she spoke, she'd crossed to a home-office setup in the corner of the room and was printing off a list of names, keeping her eye on the children and dropping in words of encouragement or censure.

"You're very good with them," said Dee enviously.

"I should be, seeing as how I was a teacher for thirty-five years and all four kids bring me their youngest spawn to look after. Retirement turned out to be an illusion. I even got a visit from social services once because I'd been reported as an unregistered child-minder!" She laughed, inviting Dee to share the joke.

"That's families for you," said Dee, making a mental note to add that to the grudges-paid list the guvnor had told her about. "Thanks for the roll call. I'll find out if anybody was ill. We have to rule out all the possibilities. Do you have contact details for the speaker?"

"Yes, of course. I tasted her stuff. It was all right, but a terrible palaver to make. Here you are, Heather Meadows. I've only got her email address, but she was very prompt about replying. Mind you, she's off on some sort of bookshop tour, so that might make a difference. We were a bit wary of asking her, to be honest, because the suggestion came from Violet and it had to be this particular month for some reason, but she's got a professional website and turned out to be on the approved WI list, so that was okay."

Dee thanked her again, noted what she herself had eaten, asked if she could hunt up who had made which cakes and escaped, reflecting that if her own mum had been anything like Julie Bamber, she'd have passed Tessa and Billy over to her to bring up as soon as they'd been weaned. Possibly even earlier.

CHAPTER TWELVE

Kenelm was on the common with the search team when Dee's text arrived. It informed him she'd got the WI attendance details, she'd emailed the speaker for the list of dishes she'd brought with her, there had been a bunch of home-made cakes that she had added to the check list, but that so far nobody had noticed what Violet ate or had been ill afterwards. He mulled this over as the line reached the far end and turned. They were working downhill in crosswise strips parallel to the line of back gardens of which Riverdene was one, and were now level with Annie's back gate. She was in the garden, ostensibly seeing to the chickens. From the grim look on her face, today's eggs were likely to reach the house curdled.

Kenelm held up his hand to pause the search. "Move down to the next position and take a five minute breather," he called. And to Annie over the fence, "You'll be delighted to hear we haven't found any hemlock yet. Nor have we trampled your squares of care."

"I know," she replied. "I was watching."

"Then why are you so cross?"

"I'm not cross. This is my normal face."

Like hell it was. "If you want cheering up, it occurred to me as we were shuffling along looking for parsley or purple spots, that if Violet's death wasn't accidental we may have to search every garden in Fencross Parva."

Annie's expression took on a tinge of awe. "Are you allowed to?"

"Not without good reason and a search warrant."

"Meaning only the gardens of people who hated her? Mine's clean if you want to lead by example. As will the Manor grounds be."

"It might come to that. I wondered about walking the dogs around the village and peering idly over fences."

She shrugged. "If it makes you happy. Just keep them away from stray cats. It wouldn't do for a policeman to be up on a breaking and entering charge. Leave that sort of thing to the chief suspect."

"One of these days you're going to say that to the wrong person. *En avant!*" he shouted to the searchers, and they continued their quartering of the common, eyes on the ground, plant identification charts in their hands.

As Kenelm moved off, Annie threw a last handful of corn down for the hens and went back to the house. *This is my normal face*, she'd said, but it wasn't. It was her the-police-are-occupying-my-common face. She hadn't realised how possessive she was. But why? It didn't bother her when people walked dogs or picnicked or played football on the common. It didn't bother her when the village fete took it over or when the school used it for sports day. Why now?

Because that was what the common was for. Those people belonged. These policemen didn't. Annie jeered at herself for being so old-Fencross and went indoors to see if Heather Meadows had emailed regarding illustrations. She knew it was unlikely, being as how she was probably in the back room of a bookshop signing copies, but hope was a terrible thing to suppress.

In which case, she decided five minutes later, pushing her chair back from an inbox devoid of financial good news – not even an internet order for a pack of birthday cards – she might as well make herself thoroughly miserable by visiting Mum. She clipped leads on Star and Sofi because sometimes they got through the fogged veil of memory even if Annie herself didn't, and walked along Mulberry Lane towards the care home. There was a barrier across the entrance to the common, warning the public to keep out. People in protective clothing were still coming and going at Riverdene. Annie reflected that it was nice for the care home residents to have something different to watch. Not Mum, though. She'd made sure Mum would have a room at the back, with a view of Clattering Road and the riding stables. The confusion of looking out from the wrong side of her own street would unbalance her completely.

In her mother's room, the dogs bounded happily to Mum who gathered as much of them as she could reach to make a fuss of. "You've been a long time getting that tea," she said. "I suppose you were painting again and forgot. I hope it was one of those nice pictures full of sunshine. I like them."

Annie's heart tugged painfully. It was evidently one of Mum's surreal days, when everything she said gave the impression of making sense, but just missed.

"You've got your tea there," she said, indicating the mug on the table drawn up next to her easy chair.

"Put it down when I wasn't looking, didn't you? Where have you been?"

Useless to explain. Just go with the flow. "I've sold a painting to the new vicar and I've been helping the police with their enquiries."

"April fool, April folly. You don't catch me like that. We haven't got a new vicar. Reverend Silver has been baptising and burying Fencross folk since Grandma was a girl."

Thanks, Mum. Query the new vicar but not the bit about me being interviewed by the police. "He retired eighteen months ago. Longer, probably. We went to his farewell party, remember? It was held outside in the churchyard and everyone was giddy with excitement at being able to talk to more than thirty people at once."

Her mother looked at her fondly but blankly.

"You must remember. The parish gave him a posh hot-chocolate maker, there was a cake in the shape of St Athelm and Minna Saxon got tipsy on the sherry."

"What sort of cake?"

"Just sponge, I think. There might have been a jam filling inside. Anyway, the new vicar's name is Rev Robin. She says she'll come and see you. You'll love her. She's got rainbow hair and a tattoo of a vine on her arm."

That produced a smile. "Get away."

"True. You wait and see. Grandma would spin in her grave. You really will like her, she was lovely to poor Minna when she was upset. Minna said she might come and see you too."

"What about Oscar? When's he coming?"

Annie's insides twisted. "Never. He left years ago and you know it. He's never coming back, Mum. All he was after was money."

Her mother looked around the room fretfully. "He sent a postcard..."

Anger burnt through her like a flame. "He didn't. He's long gone. Long, long gone. The postcard was a cruel trick by Violet Renshaw."

"Who's she?"

"The foul woman who lives in the bungalow with all the gnomes. Lived, I should say. She died yesterday. She was president of the belladonna club."

"That's Pat Williams. Who's looking after her dog if she's dead? We could have it. I like dogs." She rubbed Sofi's soft silky ears.

"It isn't Pat who died. It's Violet Renshaw, the woman I had that row with about foraging law. Dinah Gray joked that she probably used one of her own remedies."

Mum shook her head. "Not her, she knew what she was doing. You should have seen her horrid gloating face when Luke Roberts put those berries in his mouth. Turned my blood cold. She knew all right. I'm worried about the dog, Annie. You run down the road and say we'll have it."

"The dog is fine. Pat is fine. You're probably right and she's been re-elected as president already. Violet died."

"Flu, was it? The pensioner's friend. Is she a pensioner?"

"I should think so. Mind you, Jerry Ellwood has been seen visiting in the evenings again, so maybe she wasn't that old."

Mum chuckled wickedly. "That Jerry, there never was a man who needed so much dry cleaning."

Annie's lips pursed. It was Jerry who'd let the cat out of the bag about Oscar asking how much Hope Cottage would be worth. Jerry had mouthed off about it in the pub, getting in a nasty sexist dig about Oscar warming the empty-nest and he didn't suppose he was the only one being as how Margaret Dearlove was always so friendly. Gideon had overheard him and told Annie straight away. She couldn't do anything about Jerry's disgusting attitude, but she'd explained the ownership of Hope Cottage in no uncertain terms to Oscar the next weekend. He'd cleared out by the following Friday, taking Mum's dreams with him.

Mum was still talking. "Not safe in taxis, that's what Grandma would have said about him, except she never used taxis. Good fun, is Jerry, but no discrimination."

Pots and kettles, Mum, pots and kettles.

"I like fun. Shall we go to the pub? This tea's cold."

Annie picked up the mug. "They're not open. I'll make you a hot cup." She walked down the corridor to the kitchenette, wondering how much more of this she could take before she broke.

When she returned, Mum had turned the television on and was watching an antiques programme with Star's head on her lap. "That woman's got a tea set like ours," she said, pointing at the screen. "It belonged to Grandma's mother. Why don't we use it any more?"

Because Oscar sold it.

"It was too fragile," said Annie. "We packed it up and put it in the loft." And when she'd looked for it to send it to auction for the care home fees, it was gone, along with everything else of value. The loft was so empty she could probably put another Airbnb guest up there if she had any money for the conversion.

"Was that when you ran away?"

"I didn't run away. I went to art school after Grandma died, but I came home at weekends."

"You never. You ran away to go on the stage."

"That was Aunty Dora. She went to drama school."

Just for a moment there was a flash of the old rebellious spirit in Mum's face, the spirit that had brought up an illegitimate child in the face of the village's shock and Grandma's unyielding disapproval. The spirit that had charmed her into the job at the dry cleaners and propelled her out in the evenings for a vodka at the pub once Annie was in bed asleep. "She did," she said now with a crow of laughter. "We pretended she was staying with a friend. Grandma was furious. She locked me in as a punishment, but there was a fair up to Much Clattering, so I climbed out of the window on to the outhouse roof, then slid down the rainwater butt and ran all the way up the road."

Which was where she had met Annie's nameless fairground-barker father who had seduced her senseless and moved on at the end of the week. Mum was really lousy at judging men.

"Happy days," said Annie.

The irony went over her mother's head. "I like that tea set," she said. "You get it out again."

"Sure." Mum would have forgotten all about it by the end of the visit. She had a lot in common with the old porcelain. So pretty. So fragile. So easily damaged.

CHAPTER THIRTEEN

"Are you stopping for lunch, guvnor? Only I've reached Bessie from the *Cosy Kettle* on my WI meeting list."

On the other end of the phone, Dee could almost hear him wincing. "Milk it. We've nearly finished here. Total negative. I'll take the search team to the pub."

"Right. See you later."

Crossing Mulberry Lane, she noticed Annie coming out of the care home, her dogs sniffing eagerly at anything that might have changed since they went inside.

"Hi," she called, waving. "I'm on an anyone-else-ill-after-WI hunt. Minna's out, so I thought I'd combine lunch with asking Bessie what she ate at the meeting. Do you want to join me?"

Annie looked worn to the bone. She shook her head. "Not with Sofi and Star, thanks. Hygiene regulations. I had a piece of lemon drizzle cake at the meeting. Calli brought it over for me. Definitely no hemlock in it."

Dee grinned and patted the dogs who were reminding her enthusiastically that they were old friends. "None of the samples from the talk?"

"Fat chance. I was too busy selling cards to the people avoiding eating anything. Honestly, it's unlikely it happened there. Hemlock has quite a distinctive smell.

Violet might not have noticed because she always moved around in a cloud of perfume, but if one of the containers had become contaminated, Heather Meadows would have spotted it as soon as she snapped off the lid."

"Good point," said Dee, making a note. "Unless she has an irrational hatred of WI audiences, of course."

"Don't say that. She was hinting she might offer me an illustration contract."

"Go you! Real money?"

"Yup."

"Cosmic. See you later." Dee continued into the café, leaving Annie to haul the dogs past the entrance to the common.

"No," she heard her say to them. "We'll have to go via the road. I don't like it either but you can make do with the garden until Kenelm's finished. Bite his ankles when he gets back. That'll show him."

In the *Cosy Kettle*, Dee was greeted with professional caution. Evidently the word regarding hemlock had gone out.

"Hi, Bessie, I'm starving. What do you recommend for lunch today?"

The atmosphere thawed at once. "Olive's made a lovely steak-and-kidney if you'd like some?"

"I would. Oh, and I need to ask if you ate anything at the WI meeting and if you were taken ill afterwards. I'm checking everyone. Sorry." She got out her list apologetically.

"I had a piece of coffee-and-walnut cake and a cup of tea. Olive had the lemon drizzle." She lowered her voice. "Not a patch on my Nancy's. Neither of us was poorly, thank goodness. Can't run a café if you're feeling out of sorts."

"Not a very good advertisement," agreed Dee. "What about the samples from the talk?"

"We thought we'd better not, just in case."

Dee made a note. "I don't suppose you saw if Mrs Renshaw ate anything?"

Bessie shook her head. "Didn't notice her particularly until she made all that fuss at the end."

"Nor did anyone else, apparently. You're doing good business today," she added, looking at the tables. "Oh, there's Minna Saxon. I can ask her about the food and tick her off too. Who are the ladies with her?"

"Gossip hounds," said Bessie. "They're paying. The one in the purple coat is Stella Thompson. The one in black is Bonita Ellwood and the lady with the navy blazer is Hilary Myers."

"Good, I can get them all. That'll save me a tramp around. I should have come in here straight off."

Bessie nodded. "Here or Church Parade. Most locals pass through the shops during the day. You go and ask your questions. I'll set you a place at the table by the wall."

Dee headed over to where Minna had been bought another unaccustomed meal. "Hello, ladies. I'm PC Bryce. I hope you don't mind me interrupting, but I'm asking everyone who was at the WI meeting what they ate and whether they were okay afterwards. And whether anyone noticed Mrs Renshaw eating anything."

"Violet was bustling about. I had chocolate fudge cake," said the stout woman in purple. "It was so filling I couldn't manage anything else."

"Green velvet cake for me," said navy blazer.

"And me," agreed the thin, elegant woman in black. "It was delicious."

"I would have liked some of that, but it had run out by the time I got to the table," said Minna wistfully. "Your coffee-and-walnut had all gone too, Bonita. The chocolate fudge was nice though, there was plenty of that."

Dee remembered there had been a squashed piece

of chocolate cake in her fridge, along with a slice of something that could have been lemon drizzle cake. Slid into her bag when no one was looking?

She was still talking. "All the samples earlier were really lovely. I tried everything. Violet said it was a feather in our caps to have Heather as she's booked up months ahead. She told Phyllis Winterbottom to mention her name when she wrote. Oh dear, I am going to miss her. The money will be nice though. She told me she was leaving everything to me. I'll have to ask your Jerry about selling Violet's house, Bonita. I hope he can get more than he said mine was worth. It's so lovely to think I won't ever have to worry about money again." She turned to Dee. "Do you know when I can have Riverdene, dear?"

As one, her companions' eyes had whipped to Minna's guileless face. It was clear their motive in buying her lunch in order to ask about finding the body had just reaped bonus credits.

Dee replied hastily that it was nothing to do with her and it would be up to the solicitor to prove the will. "That's not always straightforward," she added, and left them to it.

"Who else have you got on your list?" asked Bessie when she served the sort of lunch that confirmed Dee's decision to bring Gran here one day.

"Not too many now. Mrs Candour, Mrs Williams, Reverend Robin."

Bessie gave a brisk nod. "Pat Williams is next door to the rectory, so if you cut up the footpath to Forge Lane from here, she's immediately opposite where you come out. Speaks as she finds, does Pat, but she's okay if you're a dog person."

Dee was definitely a dog person. As soon as Pat Williams answered the door, she was ready with her brightest smile for the silkiest creature on four legs frisking eagerly down the hall. "Oh," she said, "how gorgeous are you!"

Within moments she was being invited to accompany Pat Williams and the sweet-tempered Afghan hound on their walk to the library.

"That's very kind, but I only want to ask about the food at the WI meeting. Then I need to go next door to the rectory and find out from the vicar what she ate. I'm checking everybody."

"Vicar and her missus are out. Saw them leave a few minutes ago. Might as well talk as we walk. Shouldn't wonder if we don't catch them up. Hang on to Rupert while I shut the door."

Dee took Rupert's lead and resigned herself to a high decibel conversation the whole way to the library.

"Violet ate something she shouldn't at the meeting? Is that the idea? Wouldn't surprise me. Greediest woman I know whether it was food, friends or power. The sort who takes everything. You just ask the flower club committee. As for what I had, I tasted some of the speaker's dishes out of politeness - weren't bad - then had a slice of lemon drizzle cake with my coffee."

"No ill effects?" asked Dee.

"None. I don't hold with delicate stomachs. As long as you stick to plain British food, you'll be all right. It's when people start messing around with all this genetic modification and hidden supplements, that's when the problems start. The speaker had sensible notions, I'm glad to say, and knew a good deal about the history of rural food."

"That's useful information, thank you. I haven't had many people admitting to trying the samples."

Pat Williams gave a loud laugh. "Plenty of folk took some, but there was a fair amount left on the plates. I should know as I cleared it away. It wasn't my job to, I'm not even on the WI committee, but I'd finished mine and Phyllis Winterbottom was flapping her hands and tutting like a wet hen about the mess and how she needed to get on with the business of the meeting. The speaker was leaving early and Violet had said she'd sort the dishes out, but she'd disappeared as usual. She used to slide out of everything unless it suited her. Well, if you're a practical bod you're a practical bod and that's all there is to it. So I cleared."

"I expect they were very grateful."

"Phyllis was fussing about something else by then. Lady Honoria noticed. Told me I was a good soul and I'd get my reward in heaven even if I didn't here. Then she asked how my roses were shaping for the summer and Dinah Gray said she'd got a japonica cutting for me. Now she's what I call a proper gardener, not like some I could mention." She turned smartly down the side path to the library.

"Violet Renshaw?" said Dee innocently.

Pat produced an impressive snort as she pushed open the door. "Her! I shouldn't speak ill of the dead, but when a so-called gardener does her weeding in namby-pamby latex gloves because she doesn't want to mess her hands up... well, I know what to think. Not even proper stout gardening ones! You may well look surprised. I promise you I saw her with my own eyes just this Wednesday morning. I was dropping poor Minna Saxon off a countryside magazine I was finished with. I went down her side path thinking I'd put it on her kitchen table if she was out, and there was Violet in her back garden weeding her far border with latex gloves on. Very embarrassed of course, and inclined to be huffy about people's homes being their castles, but we old-Fencross types always use back doors and I say people shouldn't do anything in the back garden that they wouldn't in the front. Rupert, behave."

The Afghan nosed her hand briefly and trotted over to the radiator to stretch out on the carpet. Pat headed for the shelf of biographies. Slightly dazed from the barrage of talk, Dee looked across towards Calli's table and saw her chatting to a tall woman wearing jeans and a clerical collar. Next to her was a well-tailored whirlwind in floral linen.

"This is convenient," she said cheerfully to the vicar. "I need to ask what you ate at the WI meeting and whether you were okay afterwards. I'm PC Dee Bryce. I met you when we had the spot of bother last month and had to borrow the church hard-standing to park our incident van."

Rev Robin turned with a smile. "I remember. How nice to see you again. I tasted a bit of everything, then I had a piece of chocolate cake. Have you met Bunty? I'm getting her to join the library."

"And I'm saving Robin from herself. Ask any more questions quickly. We're too exposed here. We're only passing through on the way to Annie Dearlove's studio."

On the other side of the table, Calli's eyes danced. "That sounds ominous. What's up?"

"Nothing," said Robin with an indulgent smile. "We're checking out the Airbnb accommodation for when we have visitors and maybe buying more paintings for the walls."

"Don't let her fool you," said Bunty. "That's just a cover story to mask our escape. Yes, dear, I know it's your job, but you really don't need to get involved in a church hall squabble. Trust me on this."

Robin rolled her eyes. "Bunty persists in thinking I can't look after myself."

Calli chuckled. "What's the matter with the church hall?"

"It's sealed because the police need to check it. The photographic club are due to meet there tonight and are not happy. Bunty doesn't quite see why I should administer soothing syrup."

"I mean, really," said Bunty. "As if it's anything to do with her. How did they manage through eighteen months of interregnum? Before I pleaded a prior engagement for us both, there was a look in the secretary's eye that said he was about to ask if they could hold the meeting at the rectory instead."

"Don't look at me," said Calli. "I've got the reading group in here tomorrow morning. That's as much community spirit as I can muster for one week."

"My commiserations," said Bunty. "Am I registered now? Good. Over to Annie Dearlove's this minute, Robin."

"Bunty, you can't hide from my parishioners forever."

"Not forever, love, just until we've established ground rules."

"You've got to admire her," said Dee after they'd gone. "Am I all right to sit in one of your bays and write up my reports? The guvnor's meeting me here and I've got everyone now except the Manor ladies and Mrs Candour who I spy her over there in a comfy chair."

"Sure," said Calli. "Yes, Suzy brings Topsy along so she can change her book in peace, then walks her back once she's picked the kids up from school."

Topsy was quite happy to chat, telling Dee that Julie Bamber had brought over tea and lemon drizzle for both her and Lady Honoria. "I shouldn't think Dinah had a chance to eat anything. You're always too busy when you're on tea duty."

By the time the guvnor arrived, having not found any signs of hemlock on the common, Dee had nearly finished. She waited while he sent off his own report, then said quietly, "Minna Saxon was in the *Cosy Kettle*, being bought lunch by a group of ladies. She was full of plans for Riverdene."

He made a face. "She hasn't got a hope. The will won't stand up without a signature and witnesses."

"Poor Minna. All that motive for people to gossip about and not even any reward to make up for it. Hardly seems fair."

"Violet Renshaw embraced unfairness. You ask Annie. Where's your report?"

At his tense tone she decided a tactical retreat was in order. "Here, sir. All checked except the Manor ladies. I'll make us a coffee, shall I, while you ring them? Calli won't mind."

CHAPTER FOURTEEN

He really *didn't* deserve Dee. Kenelm ran his eye over the results of her enquiries while he thawed out and sipped his coffee. "Did anyone notice if Violet ate any of the samples?" Even as he asked he remembered with a nasty jab his mother saying Violet had taken the largest piece of the cake she herself was cutting.

"Not that they told me. My impression is everyone helped themselves to the speaker's dishes. Mrs Candour said your mother was on tea duty, but I don't know what that entailed." Her voice was studiously neutral.

"Cutting cake and pouring out tea, apparently. In which case the meeting is a washout as far as intent-to-harm goes. Nobody could guarantee which spoonful of this or that Violet tried, nor which piece of cake."

"Pat Williams says she was greedy."

Which everyone would have known. And his mother's voice again: *easily the largest piece of cake*. Disquiet sharpened his tone. "It's still impossible. If someone had sprinkled chopped hemlock on to my lemon drizzle, I think I'd notice."

"Me too, but what if it was green velvet cake?"

The world suddenly flashed nightmare negative in front of his eyes. *That* was what his mother had been cutting.

He kept his face impassive with considerable effort. "My mother mentioned that. She was slicing it. I assumed it was just a name, like carrot cake or Madeira cake. Is it really green?"

"So I'm told."

"Wonderful. Who brought it to the meeting?"

"I'll ring Julie Bamber. She was sorting me out a list of who provided what."

Green velvet cake. This week of all weeks. And no doubt decorated all over, so a sprinkle of finely chopped hemlock on a single slice wouldn't be noticed. He listened to Dee's murmured conversation with painful intensity.

"*Nancy's Fancies* provided the green velvet cake," she reported. "Normally the WI frown on anything not homemade, but it was Moira O'Hara's birthday and she'd loved the cakes Nancy made for St Patrick's Day this year, so she ordered a large one for the meeting as her contribution to the refreshments. I asked Julie Bamber how many people might have known there was going to be a green velvet cake."

"Go on," said Kenelm fatalistically.

"Julie says Moira told *everyone* of the treat in store."

"And it's really green?"

Dee extracted a business card from one of her pockets. "Green, with shamrocks and sprinkles and all sorts on it. Bessie gave me this the other day. I still don't see how anyone could have doctored one slice."

Kenelm took the card and flipped it over. There was a display of Nancy's cakes on the reverse. One of them was indisputably green. "Great. You'd better type that up for Macready as well."

While she did so, he read the superintendent's latest missive. At the far end of the room, Calli and Gideon were shepherding the final stragglers out of the library.

"How's it going?" Calli asked, coming across and

dropping into a chair once the bolt was pulled firmly across.

"The bungalow is clean," said Kenelm. "The common is clean. The search team have moved across to the church hall and Macready is disgruntled as hell."

"Why?"

"Because with no trace of hemlock at Riverdene, it is looking possible that Violet was poisoned at the WI meeting by person or persons unknown, went home - slightly giddy, according to Minna, which would fit - had a shouting match with Annie and died overnight. Macready thinks this is unnecessarily messy and complicates a nice case of accidental death."

Calli looked unconvinced. "I had the impression hemlock was fast acting."

"You've been reading the wrong poems. Onset can be between twenty minutes and a couple of hours according to the experts. Macready is waiting for the hall results, then he wants to see everyone who was anywhere near each blessed morsel Violet ate. Which set of people, amusingly, includes my mother who cut her a nice piece of green cake. With scattered decorations on."

Calli nodded. "I avoided that one. Something very wrong with green cake. I had the chocolate fudge."

"I wish bloody Violet had."

"I have to hand it to you, Kenelm," said Gideon. "You don't do things by halves. Last month you were managing a murder scene where two of your cousins were suspects. This week the victim is a woman your mother and your landlady were threatening to tear limb from limb."

"Some of us," said Kenelm bitterly, "are naturally talented."

Calli made a sympathetic face. "If it's any comfort, I don't see how Dinah could know which piece of cake Violet would take. There was an awful lot of determined angling for position around that end of the refreshment table. Even Bonita Ellwood, who is the thinnest woman I've ever seen, did a first-day-of-the-sales rush. She was jabbing her elbows everywhere to get to her slice of green velvet, including into Violet's ribs. I daresay Violet would have added that to the grudge list if she'd lived another day."

Gideon frowned. "It might be worth matching Violet's ticks against people who were at the meeting. I find it difficult to believe anyone in Fencross Parva would go to the length of killing her for calling in the RSPCA or bringing down the tax inspectors, but they might have wanted to cause her some discomfort as a pay-back measure and didn't realise how strong hemlock was. Has Macready worked out what the list means yet?"

"I haven't been informed. I only get actions, not the thought processes behind them." He glanced across to Dee. "If you've finished, get away home. At least tomorrow's case conference is at Riverdene, not at the station."

"Let me know how it goes. I've got the weekend off." She picked up her hat, her brow wrinkling. "Why is it called Riverdene anyway? There's no river anywhere near here, is there?"

Kenelm exchanged a considering look with Gideon. "Not a river, no. Fencross brook runs along the edge of the common on Annie's side. Then it tunnels under the lane and carries on beside the footpath towards Much Clattering. It doesn't go near the bungalows."

"Weird. I'll pop in on Minna Saxon and ask her."

"If you can catch her at home," said Calli. "Being a celebrity is doing splendid things for her social life."

Dee buttoned her notebook away and brushed herself down. "She was in the café earlier. I know what you mean about that thin woman. She was there too. She almost disappears when she turns sideways, doesn't she? I can see why people think her husband might play away. That's assuming the estate agent Minna was at pains to tell me wasn't a special friend of Violet's is her husband not her brother or cousin or something?"

"Bonita and Jerry Ellwood, yes," said Gideon. "Jerry has wandering hands, but is very careful to keep the fact from Bonita."

"Hence the *JE 27 mins* entry in the notebook?" said Calli. "Potential blackmail material?"

"Could be," agreed Gideon.

Dee nodded. "That's what I guessed. Anyway, Minna will be back by now to feed the cat even if she's too full of other people's bribery to cook for herself. I've got to go past there to get to the car."

"Are you serious about asking her?" said Kenelm.

"It's bugging me, guvnor."

"I'll walk with you, then you can drop me off at Ellwood's shop on New Parade. Macready picked up that evening-visit from your conversation with Bessie from the café. I'm to interview him regarding his movements on Wednesday night. Failing accidental death, Macready likes nothing better than an extra-marital affair as a motive. I'll check the bungalow is secure before we go, being as how we haven't yet got anyone to release it to."

Dee's face registered surprise. "Still? Macready's slipping."

"His *team* is slipping. He's raging. The bank are playing hard to get and he's never before come across a one-man-band solicitor who packs up and goes on a fortnight's climbing holiday with no access to the internet."

Gideon laughed. "Violet must have used Fortescue. He's back next week. I wonder why she chose someone local to here, not wherever she was before?"

"That's word for word what Detective Superintendent Macready said. Except he included more expletives. He can't find any reason for her to have gone into hiding, so he's taking her woman-of-mystery act as a personal affront. See you tomorrow, Calli. Thanks for the use of the library."

"No problem."

"Drop in to the Lodge later if you like," said Gideon. "I'll be in. Calli's having a zoom call with her friend Meriel. It goes on for hours."

"Thanks. I might do that."

Calli looked at him seriously. "Have you thought it could be a good thing Violet hid herself? If she was as nasty at her last address as she's been here, you'd double the number of people irritated enough to take a swipe at her."

Kenelm felt thoroughly fed up. "Spiffing. I can see tomorrow's actions being to organise a door-to-door of everyone in Fencross Parva, asking if Violet ever mentioned a previous place of residence."

Naturally, once voiced, the idea failed to go away. He walked to Riverdene mentally planning exactly that operation.

"Just like being on the beat, isn't it?" said Dee, breaking the silence. "But without the rough sleepers and the county-line kids with pockets full of drugs to keep an eye open for."

"Are you saying Fencross is boring?"

"It's nice for a change, but it doesn't keep you on your toes. It's not real life, is it?"

"Don't let Gideon hear. His theory is that a village is a microcosm of society."

"Wouldn't suit me. Give me a city any day."

"You might live longer here than in the city."

She grinned. "Only if you stay off the vegetation. Here we are. Are you coming in to see Minna?"

"Worried you might need back-up?"

She chuckled, then straightened her face as the door opened. "Hi, Minna. I'm about to go off-duty and thought I'd check how you were getting on first."

"Oh, that's thoughtful, dear. People are being very kind. I haven't had to make a single meal yet. They will keep talking about Violet though. I miss her dreadfully." She peered in the direction of the next-door bungalow. "It's quite comforting in a way, having the police at Riverdene. Makes you feel more secure. You read so much about break-ins, don't you, and with those tramps sometimes sleeping rough in the old stables at the end of the road... well, it's worrying."

"We aim to please," said Dee cheerfully. "How did it come to be called Riverdene? It's a pretty name."

Minna gave an eager smile. "It is, isn't it? Violet brought the name board with her from her old house. It looks so smart and had cost quite a bit, so she wanted to carry on using it."

"I don't blame her. Where was she before, then?"

"I don't know, dear. Somewhere on the other side of Ely. I did ask, but she was really much more interested in talking about Fencross Parva and the people here, because she wanted to belong to the village like I do. Violet was so interested in people. She liked to know about everyone's families, who had large ones, who was all alone, who had children. During lockdown she was worried about all the people who might be lonely. Did they have friends to phone them, that sort of thing. She was quite envious of me because she said I knew everyone. Which I do, of course."

"It's good to have roots," agreed Dee. "I won't keep you. Timmy will be wanting his tea."

"That," said Kenelm, once the door was safely shut, "was sheer genius about the name board. I'll add it to my report, giving you full credit."

"Nosiness has its uses, sir, even if it's only for muddying the water. Shall I come with you to see this womanising estate agent rather than just dropping you off? It makes it look more official."

"Not to mention taking you nicely into an extra hour of overtime," said Kenelm in his driest voice.

"I'll try to bear up," said Dee cheerfully.

CHAPTER FIFTEEN

If Jerry Ellwood was surprised to be visited by two officers of the law, you would never have known it from his welcome. He ushered them convivially into his office, summed up Kenelm's buying power in a glance, shot Dee a practised look of admiration which she received with polite incredulity, and asked Kenelm how he could help. "If you are looking to relocate to the village, there are one or two properties you might be interested in." He gave a chummy man-to-man laugh. "Not as grand as Fencross Manor, I'm afraid, but very desirable."

Kenelm felt his hackles rise at the man's familiarity and instructed them to behave. "I'm here on police business, Mr Ellwood. We are looking into the death of Mrs Violet Renshaw. I understand you were on friendly terms with her?"

Still with a smile on his face, the estate agent contrived to back pedal rapidly on the here-to-help-you bonhomie. "I like to stay on good terms with all my clients, Inspector. You never know when people are going to up-size. Or downsize."

"Very commendable. Even to the extent of calling on them in the evenings on the way to the fish and chip shop, I hear," said Kenelm pleasantly. "We have a witness."

The grin became a trifle fixed. "Mrs Renshaw asked me for a current valuation. It was to do with her insurance."

Kenelm had an excellent memory. He clearly recollected Violet Renshaw's bank statement as showing an insurance premium going out a good six months ago. "Is that so? Odd time of night to choose," he said.

"That was when she asked me to call. In my line of business, appointments are always at the convenience of the client."

"But she wasn't a client. It was six years ago that she bought her bungalow through your agency. You were contacted by a member of the investigative team just yesterday for her previous address, but said you never kept past details on file."

"Once a client, always a client, Inspector," he said suavely. "Data protection is a different issue."

They could go round in circles like this forever. "Exemplary. As you are no doubt aware, we have to follow up all lines of enquiry. Purely as a matter of routine, would you mind telling me what your movements were on Wednesday?"

"Wednesday? Let me see, that was my wife's WI night. She ate early and left me a plate of chicken salad in the fridge. I ate it while I caught up on paperwork. Quite a tricky contract as a matter of fact. I was still at it when Bonita got home. Then I was in the doghouse for not putting my plate in the dishwasher. Women, eh? We had a glass of wine and watched television, then turned in."

The girl from the outer office came into the room, looking apologetic. "Sorry to bother you, Jerry, but Mrs Ameeter has locked herself out again. Can I sign for the spare and I'll let her in on my way home. I'll bring it back tomorrow."

"Thank you, Lorna. That will be quite in order." He pulled out a drawer in the filing cabinet, selected a folder with a practised hand and produced a key and a release form.

The young woman scrawled her name, said "See you tomorrow," and left. A moment later they heard the shop door bang.

"A service we provide to past clients," explained Jerry.

Kenelm stood up. "Useful, no doubt. If there are any other questions, you'll be contacted. We'll see ourselves out."

"Ugh," said Dee once they were on the pavement.

"Indeed. Interesting exchange at the end. Do people not have neighbours with spare keys any more? Gideon would be horrified."

"Not ones she trusts, maybe. Mrs Ameeter is in Church Lea. I remember her from last time. She's the one that told us about all the comings and goings and shouting matches in the road. Don't think there's much love lost between her and her neighbours."

"That explains it. Even so, I do wonder how many other keys Jerry Ellwood happens to have held on to. I'll add it to my report. Off you go. I'll walk back. I need to shake off the grease."

For once, the kitchen at Hope Cottage was empty. Kenelm had learnt enough in his fortnight's tenure not to disturb Annie when she was in her studio, so he went upstairs to change and have a hot shower while no one else was likely to be affected by a potential power surge from the water heater. At some point he and Annie were going to have to have a discussion regarding best practice for electrical appliances and just who had been induced to write her out a safety certificate. He might wait for her to be in a good mood first.

As he towelled himself dry, he looked around his

room, at its mix of furniture, erratic placement of plug sockets and the view through the window of Church Lea, the crowded estate on what had used to be a wide green remnant of meadow around the church. Displacement gnawed at him. Fencross Parva was his natal village, yet nothing in this room was familiar, nothing said home. Even the shape of St Athelm's tower was different from this side. He felt untethered, as if he'd missed a step in the dark. Where *was* home for him now? Jerry Ellwood's jibe about relocation brushed across him like sandpaper on an open wound.

Below, he heard the dogs barking. That meant Annie was in the kitchen. He dressed and went down to make himself a coffee. It was horribly craven, needing Sofi's and Star's pleasure in seeing him to make himself feel better, but at least he could offer to take them for a walk as compensation.

To his surprise, Annie donned boots and an anorak and came too.

"Don't you have to wait in for the new visitors?" he asked.

"I'm not going to be long. I need some air and time to think. God, I really hate not being free to do what I like."

He gave a twisted smile. "And there was me feeling the exact opposite."

Her gaze under her dark fringe was frank and direct. "Your old life, you mean? Do you *want* to go back?"

Did he? "No, not really," he said, to his own surprise. "It couldn't ever be the same, not after all Sarah's said. I just want this interim limbo to be over. I want to fast-forward to a settled state. I'm not very good at change."

"How do you cope with your job, then?" she asked. "You said each day could be different, that you got on with what you were given. That sounds pretty erratic."

"Work is a different beast. It's a challenge. The variety

prevents me getting stale or complacent. Each assignment involves a new set of factors to work with." He tried to find a parallel. "I suppose it's a bit like the way each new painting you do is something unique, not a copy of the one before. That's fine for the day job, but I can't live like it twenty-four-seven. When I'm off-duty I want stability, something unquestioned." He paused. "Something that's mine."

Annie was silent for a moment, watching the dogs frisking ahead. "The separation must be difficult for the kids."

He gave a short laugh. "It's a nightmare. Tom is angry with both of us. He's the eldest. He'll text me, but not talk. Rick is just upset."

"Poor beggars. I wouldn't be a teenager again. Emotions bubbling away and you've no idea how to control them. You know so much, and yet you're helpless. They must be feeling like you. They're changing so much inside they want everything outside to stay the same, just for balance."

"It wasn't my choice to leave." That was said too fast, too bitterly. He took a deep breath. "It would have come to it though," he admitted. "Sarah and I were tearing each other apart. That wasn't good for the boys either."

"Bring them over here if you want, so they can see where you're living and have a run on the common with you and the dogs. It might help."

Kenelm was touched. "Thank you."

She hunched her shoulders irritably. "I was a stroppy adolescent once. It was only painting that got me through. That and your mother teaching me about plants."

They'd reached the purple fence. Kenelm eyed it with dislike. "I won't be sorry to release this place. Dee asked Minna about the name Riverdene, by the way. Violet brought the board with her from her previous house. Didn't want to waste what she'd paid good money for. I'll put it in the report for Macready this evening. I'm trying to decide whether to do a search on every Riverdene in Cambridgeshire, past and present, or whether to leave tracing Violet to the police computer."

Annie pulled Star away from the purple fence. "Is it your job?"

"No, but the more efficient I am, the less likely it is that I'll be reassigned."

"Does that matter?"

He spoke without thinking. "It does when you and my mother are prominent amongst the suspects."

He felt her start of surprise, but she covered it in true Annie fashion. "Why the hell are you hanging around here then? Go and start searching."

"Yes, ma'am." He braced himself. "It would be easier if I wasn't so concerned about fusing the electrics every time I plug in a new device. There's a limit to the number of multi-gang sockets one outlet will safely take. Would you object if I got an electrician to put another couple of sockets in my room? I'll pay."

Sarah would have taken any such remark about the inadequacies of her home as a criticism. Annie looked mildly puzzled that he was worried. "Sure. Provided they don't burn the place down."

As this was precisely Kenelm's fear every time he charged his phone, he clamped his teeth on his immediate reply. "Don't say that when they're here or they'll slap an emergency call-out charge on the bill. I'll ask Gideon who he recommends."

Annie nodded. "Talking of Gideon, if you want him to give you a hand shifting furniture out of your room so you can bring in stuff from home or the Manor, I don't mind. It might help to make it feel more familiar."

It was Kenelm's turn to be startled. "Thank you. That's really kind."

"No it's not. It's easier to have you settled in than it is to keep letting the damn room out to more bastard visitors."

As they started back, Minna Saxon's kitchen door opened. A black shape stalked down the path, accompanied by a timid exhortation to be a good cat. Sofi and Star immediately surged to the wire netting with a volley of barks.

"Quiet, idiot hounds," said Annie, hauling on their leads. "Home. Food."

The cat sat down and washed unhurriedly. It was difficult not to think he was doing it on purpose. In the midst of the noise, Annie's phone gave an insistent trill.

"Give me the dogs," said Kenelm, reaching for the leads. "You'll tie yourself in knots."

"Hello, we're here," squawked the phone. "There's no one to let us in."

"Visitors," muttered Annie with loathing. Into the phone, she said, "I'll be with you in a few minutes. You're earlier than you said you'd be."

"I don't think so," came the offended voice. "Foul journey. I'm desperate for a shower and a chamomile tea."

"Another guest doomed to disappointment," murmured Kenelm.

Annie thumbed the phone off. "Shut up. It says on the website to bring stuff with them. God, I hate visitors. Bunty was over this afternoon talking about the big canvas she has in mind for their sitting room wall. I want to paint it like you wouldn't believe, but when the hell am I going to find time and head space for something that size? I'm so sick of being sensible. I feel like that Greek bloke who had to push a boulder uphill all the time for no damn reason. Except... maybe I do deserve it because of moving Mum to the care home and not looking after her myself."

"You're kidding," said Kenelm in honest disbelief. "You feel guilty for sacrificing your work - sacrificing who you are - in order to make sure your mother can have the best standard of care possible? That's plain ridiculous, Annie."

"It's a nice way of putting it."

"Its true. Stop wallowing in guilt. Where does that come from? Your grandma?"

"Yup. Thou shalt not enjoy yourself. Life is hard. Deal with it."

"Don't be absurd. You are your own person. Use your talents. It's really not a sin."

"Bloody difficult when you've had a lifetime of conditioning."

"Sarah tells me women have inbuilt remorse. You don't usually conform to type. Can't you close your bookings and forget about visitors for a fortnight if you need time to paint? Will Bunty pay enough to cover the loss of rent?"

A look of utter astonishment crossed Annie's face. She brushed her hair out of the way and stared at him. "She will. Dear Lord in heaven, where is my brain these days? I never even thought of doing that. You're a genius." Then, as her phone trilled again, "Not *again*. Shut up. I'm on my way."

Kenelm grinned. "Go and sort them out. I'll give the dogs a bit longer."

"Cheers. Bloody visitors." She stomped off.

Kenelm strolled slowly on, enjoying the evening, enjoying Sofi and Star investigating each new blade of grass, each patch of thistles. His gaze slid over the other houses backing on to the common. There hadn't been a flicker of interest from any of them when the dogs were barking earlier. If he brought the boys over, they'd be able to race around and make as much noise as they liked. Sarah was always saying the neighbours complained when they kicked footballs about in the garden with their mates. Seeing them here *would* settle him. It would stop him feeling so detached. The rest of his things would help too. Not furniture, that belonged in Sarah's house. It was airy and modern, suited to a middle-class semi on the outskirts of Ely, not a three-hundred year old cottage with twisting staircases and a Sleeping Beauty garden. Nor did he want to bring anything over from the Manor, though heaven knows they had stuff from every conceivable era to spare. The only room he'd ever coveted in the Manor had been his father's study.

A desk, though... Gideon could make him a good solid desk for the end wall, with shelves above for all his books, space for photos of the boys. Something that was purely his. Something to tether him.

As he reached Annie's back gate, St Athelm's clock chimed the hour. The mellow notes fell into his head with the familiarity of belonging. He didn't know whether to laugh or cry. He'd thought he'd grown away from Fencross Parva. It was bittersweet to realise it hadn't believed him.

CHAPTER SIXTEEN

Kenelm sat back from his laptop. "On average, how many houses called Riverdene would you say there are in Cambridgeshire?"

Gideon returned him a shrewd look. One of the many things that had annoyed Kenelm in the old days was how his cousin had worn his intelligence so lightly. Now he was grateful. Gideon was a safe outlet for his irritation. Anything he raged at in the safety of the Lodge would go no further. Tonight, for instance, Gideon had made no comment when Kenelm had taken up his offer and appeared at his back door, saying the latest batch of visitors were infesting Annie's place and was it okay if he sat at the table here and did some online searches? He had simply waved him to a chair. Now he cleared the debris from his whittling of chess pieces out of the way and said, "I'm guessing more than one?"

"Five. The amusing thing is three of them used to belong to Violet Renshaw."

"That's interesting."

"Isn't it just. I have forwarded the info to Macready, who is probably aware of it already, having obtained her details from the bank, but didn't consider I needed to be informed." Kenelm kept his voice level.

"This would be the same Macready who has done nothing about Violet's nasty little ways regarding the spying on of neighbours? The plain clothes team must have worked out what the notebook entries mean by now, surely."

"You'd think. Again, I might not have been informed. I'm not sure his heart is in this case enough to bother analysing Violet's character. He probably just thinks she moved around a lot." Kenelm frowned at his screen. "Which she evidently did. I could bear to know why. Dee made a valid point that it was odd to choose an unknown area. Was that the case every time? Violet doesn't change her name, so it isn't witness relocation. It has to be her activities. She makes herself too unpopular to stick around, so she moves on."

"Cutting all ties in case one of her victims of malicious gossip tracks her and bumps her off?"

"That would be one inference."

Gideon scrubbed a hand through his hair. "No, it won't work. She wasn't that bothered if she kept the same house name each time. Anyone could search for it as you did and find her current address easily."

"So she if wasn't in hiding, why move? Looking for new friends?"

"Seems unlikely, as she didn't care about the ones she made. She never kept in touch. She didn't concern herself being polite or worry about what they thought of her. She didn't have any fond memories to recall."

Kenelm felt a sense of profound dissatisfaction. He lifted a hand and let it drop. "And then there's hemlock. I mean, just how? I told you we didn't find any on the common, didn't I?"

"You did. Nor in her bungalow. Anything in the church hall?"

"Not so far. Macready's livid because it expands the

scope and cuts into his budget. He's got his team checking on suspicious packages sent through the mail or surprise dainty tartlets left on the doorstep tied up with ribbon. The point for me is hemlock is so arcane. It's an offence against police investigation."

Gideon put a wedge of Stilton, a box of biscuits and a bottle of wine on the table. "What it is, is specific. Somebody in Violet's circle knew the effect, knew how to get hold of the plant, knew how to use it and didn't think they'd be caught."

"So, start with my mother and Annie and work onwards from there?"

Gideon added glasses, plates and knives. "Stop being negative. Calli's made a lovely list of suspects from the notebooks."

"I prefer negative. You never get a nasty surprise. I ought to congratulate Dee on the Riverdene idea. I might as well send her the list of addresses so she can feel properly gratified." He began typing on his phone.

"Won't tomorrow do?"

"She's got the weekend off." He paused. "Also she has good insights. There is potentially a killer in Fencross Parva. I'm not going to give up until they've been collared." *Oh God, he'd said it. He'd admitted this was his village.* He changed the subject abruptly, nodding towards the basket of chess pieces. "You make nice things."

"Thank you. I don't like waste, even of odds and ends of wood. I market them as reclaimed chess sets and they sell surprisingly well."

"I'm in awe of anyone with a talent. Did I tell you Dee's husband just had to listen to my engine and he knew what was wrong and how to fix it?"

"Cultivate him. Someone who understands cars is worth their weight in gold."

"Trust me, I am." Kenelm picked up a pawn from the

basket, amused to see the faint suggestion of a police constable's helmet incised on it. "If I stay lodging at Annie's, will you make me a desk and shelves for the end wall of my room?"

"Sure. Family rates, I assume?"

"That would be helpful." He got out another policeman-pawn and tried to see what Gideon had done to give them character. "These are clever. I've never been able to slow down enough for craft work."

His cousin threw him an ironic look. "You organise the people who keep us safe. Don't beat yourself up. You can't do everything." He poured wine into both glasses. "Welcome home, mate."

Dee read the guvnor's text for a second time and looked speculatively over to where her husband was stretched full length along the settee, supposedly watching the snooker, actually four-fifths asleep.

"Eithan..." she said.

That's me," he replied lazily.

"It's my day off tomorrow."

"I know. You are going to make bacon sandwiches. You are going to make all of us bacon sandwiches. I've bought the bacon and the bread and everything."

"That's on Sunday. I'm making bacon sandwiches on Sunday."

"With ketchup."

"With ketchup. *Tomorrow*, when we go to see Gran for her birthday before we dump the kids at their Taekwon Do class..."

"Cancelled. Some bastard torched the leisure centre."

"I'd forgotten. We'll have to find somewhere else to wear them out. Anyway, when we go to see Gran..."

He opened one eye. "Yes?"

"It's just... if it sounds as if I'm asking her some odd questions, don't worry about it. It's still my day off. I'm not working."

He closed the eye again. "You were a copper when I met you, babe. You were a copper when I married you."

She grinned. "Struck lucky, didn't I?"

"Nah, that was me when you immobilised that bloke who was trying to glass me. Neatest move I ever saw. She's a keeper, I thought, as I finished my beer."

Dee stretched out a leg and nudged him affectionately. "Your ma should have stopped you growing when you were younger. Anyone six foot four with the wrong colour skin in the boozer on a Saturday night is asking for trouble." She took a last look at the guvnor's text before turning the screen off. It probably wouldn't come to anything. Sutton was a fair-sized place. The chance of Gran knowing anything about a woman who had lived in a house called Riverdene in Sutton over six years ago was vanishingly small, but there was no harm in trying, was there?

"Right," snarled Detective Superintendent Macready at the case meeting on Saturday morning at Riverdene. "No packages through the mail or any of the main courier services. Nothing in the church hall. This house is cleaner than a hospital operating theatre and yet hemlock entered the deceased's digestive system and bloody well killed her. Where did it come from? She wasn't universally liked, being inquisitive and abrasive, but there's no evidence of blackmail because the only significant additions to her bank account in recent years happened whenever she moved."

"Lucky woman," grumbled the head of the forensics team. "When I moved it cost *me* money."

"She was planning on another relocation," put in the

detective sergeant sitting next to Macready, "judging by her Internet searches and the mini-cab company she used. Their drivers all say she had a list of addresses in various Cambridgeshire villages and wanted the cabs to cruise slowly around looking at them."

Kenelm didn't point out that there were other forms of blackmail than monetary ones. The superintendent wouldn't have listened anyway. He was talking again, raking the small group around Violet's dining table with a sarcastic glare.

"What the hell do I keep you all on the payroll for? I can see the bloody grass growing on you. An amateur herbalist is dead from something she ate within the last twelve hours of her life. It's not rocket science. I want a minute by minute timetable of that meeting at the church hall. I want every garden in this damn village searched for hemlock. I want the rubbish tip turned over inch by inch until her personal black refuse sack is found with the remains in it of her last meal." He drew a breath. "However, due to manpower and budget restrictions, I'll settle for remote checks on her previous addresses for anyone nearby with form, investigating that estate agent's alibi for the evening and I also want to question the neighbour again about every movement the deceased made for the last week of her life. Ask her to step in here, Inspector."

Kenelm left him delegating tasks to his team and took himself smartly next door. No one answered his knock. On the windowsill, the cat watched disdainfully. "I don't suppose you know where she is?" he asked. "What happens in Fencross Parva at ten o'clock on a Saturday morning?"

The cat ignored him. He rang his mother.

"Reading group, darling. It's in the library today because your people are still occupying the church hall. Can you hurry them up at all? The church coffee rota is getting het-up about tomorrow. I don't know why these wretched people think I can do anything about it, but I said I'd ask."

He cast his eyes briefly upwards. There was a poisoner at large in the village, yet the prime concern of the Friends of St Athelm was where they would have coffee after the morning service. "I'll see what I can do."

At the library, Calli was also looking restive. "I swear this reading group makes more noise than a dozen children's story-time sessions put together."

The bay nearest the door was certainly very disorderly. "What are they reading?" asked Kenelm. "I didn't think you had anything that contentious on the shelves."

"I haven't, not ones they've all read. 'Reading group' is an elastic term. Today they are discussing this week's *People's Friend* magazine. There has been considerable disagreement on what counts as store-cupboard staples."

"If any of them mention hemlock, let me know. Meanwhile, I've come to take Minna Saxon off your hands. Macready wants to see her again."

"That's no help," said Calli. "Minna hardly says a word. Take Bonita or Pat." She winced as a particularly loud outburst on the subject of Japanese breadcrumbs reached them. "Or both. Take them both."

"Sadly, my instructions are solely for Minna."

While Kenelm waited for Calli to extract her, a well-dressed woman with a bony, eager face walked in and came up to the counter. She looked around and turned to him with a smile. "Sorry to bother you, but is the librarian about?"

"She'll be back in a moment."

"Thank you. I'm trying to find an address in the village and I hoped there might be a local directory here. The woman I'm looking for is a divine illustrator. Like a fool, I gave her card to my agent, who has managed to take a tumble down some steps and break not only her leg, poor soul, but also my laptop. I don't suppose you know an artist hereabouts called Annie Dearlove? I'm desperate to get in touch. She must think I'm so rude for not having done so already. I tried her website but my phone is so old it can't manage, so when I realised Fencross Parva was on my way home, I pulled in on the off-chance of locating her."

Kenelm just managed to stop his jaw dropping. "I do know Annie Dearlove, yes. You wouldn't be Heather Meadows by any chance?"

The woman's face broke into a delighted smile. "I am! Goodness, aren't our police wonderful. However did you know?"

What a stroke of luck. He could get the list of dishes and ingredients, check on the serving of them and cross another action off Macready's list.

"My name is Inspector Gray. I've been trying to get in touch with you. I wonder if I might ask a few questions? It's about the talk you gave in the church hall on Wednesday night. I'd like a list of the dishes you made and the ingredients that went into them."

"Yes, of course. I have them on my home computer. I can email them as soon as I get back." Her face changed. "Oh goodness, was someone allergic? I do always ask."

Calli returned with a flustered Minna Saxon. The bay had fallen silent. At least two noses were poking around the corner.

"Oh, it's Heather Meadows," cried Minna, disastrously audible for once. "Hello. Isn't it sad about poor Violet?"

Heather's attention sharpened. "Violet? Violet Renshaw? What about her?"

"She's passed away. Isn't it dreadful?"

"*Violet?*"

Kenelm threw a fulminating look at Minna, then turned back to Heather. "I *have* left several messages for you."

"I was getting a very poor signal, sorry, and then with the lap-top breaking... Dear me, this changes all my plans for today. I'd better ring my husband to tell him I'll be delayed. The poor man will be forgetting what I look like."

"I doubt we'll be long," said Kenelm, somewhat taken aback. "It's just the list of dishes I need. It's a question of elimination."

"It's rather more than that, Inspector. Violet Renshaw was my half-sister. I'm her next-of-kin."

Kenelm hardly heard the incredulous gasps from the reading group. Violet Renshaw had a sister? Bloody hell, this altered everything. Macready was going to want to question her for sure. He opened his mouth to speak, but before he could put a polite request to accompany him to Riverdene into words, Minna had cut across both of them with a piercing scream.

"No! No, you can't be. She would have told me. We were talking about you. She would have told me."

Heather shook her head apologetically. "She never told anyone. It was one of her foibles. She preferred people to think she was alone in the world. Oh dear, I'll have to contact my solicitor."

"If that's also the solicitor who acted for Mrs Renshaw on personal matters, then I wish you would," said Kenelm. "I need someone to release the bungalow to. Can you give me the contact details?"

"Certainly, I have them at home. Is there an email address I can use for you? You can release her house to me straight away if you like. I'm Violet's executor and principal legatee."

The whole reading group was now in the main room, utterly engrossed. There was a buzz of surprise at Heather's words, overlaid by a further wail of anguish from Minna.

"But she left everything to me. We did the wills together. It's all mine."

Thank God Macready wasn't here to hear confirmation in front of a crowd of witnesses that Minna had expected to scoop the lot. It never failed to astound Kenelm what little sense of self-preservation people had.

"Oh heavens, I'm so sorry," said Heather helplessly. "Isn't that just like her? It's not true, my dear, and she should never have let you think so. Violet wasn't always... she wasn't always very kind."

"The will form in her drawer isn't signed or witnessed, Miss Saxon," Kenelm confirmed in an apologetic voice.

Minna stared blankly at them both and burst into huge, messy tears. The reading group regarded him with considerable censure.

Great. Wonderful. Now he was going to be accused of police brutality.

Calli put her arm around Minna's convulsively shuddering shoulders. "Do you want to take Ms Meadows to Riverdene to talk to the detective in charge?" she said to Kenelm. "You can come back for Minna. She'll be calmer after a cup of tea."

He nodded. Macready would no doubt give him hell for not turning on the third-degree before the effect of the shock had worn off, but there were limits to what he could stomach. "Thank you. I'll do that."

Heather Meadows made a restraining movement. "Wait. Annie Dearlove. I simply must contact her."

"You want Annie? I'll phone her," said Calli.

"You angel. Can you ask her to bring around another business card? Thank you so much. I'll pop back later."

Kenelm sent Calli an *I'm trusting you* look that he wasn't entirely sure she understood, then left with Heather Meadows who was asking in a warm voice if she was allowed to drive him to Riverdene and free up one of the library's parking spaces. He assented absently. If he'd probed his own feelings, he would have discovered he was feeling hopeful. Nice as she seemed, a half-sister who was the principal legatee and a wild forager into the bargain would certainly take the heat off Annie and his mother as suspects.

CHAPTER SEVENTEEN

Gran had opened her birthday presents, approved the kids' home-made cards and tucked away the bottles and chocolates for later when she didn't have to share with anyone. Now she looked up alertly at Dee's question.

"Violet Renshaw? Of course I remember her, I'm not senile. All mouth and sugar-coating, that was her. It was a while ago, mind. She wasn't here for long. Iris Marks pegged her for a nosy parker because she wanted to know everything about everybody. She was a show-off too. Nice garden if all you want is flowers, but she couldn't grow a row of runner beans to save her life. It was a right laugh when she moved. The couple who bought her house could have gone for two or three from that terrace - all ex-council, so about the same price - but they picked hers because of the garden. Then when they moved in they found she'd dug up half the plants and taken them with her. Laugh, we nearly died."

"Charming. Why did she move away?"

"Never settled. Tried one friend then another. Came down to the lunch club at the Flag now and again, but not regularly, said the portions were too small. When it closed because of all that bother with the mouse droppings and the food inspectors, the pub took over the lunch club so she didn't come at all. She didn't get on with Jackie. Not many do, but when it's your local you've got to support it, haven't you?"

"You do if you want a pensioner's special every Wednesday and a half-price gin afterwards," said Dee. "What had she got against Jackie?"

"All sorts. Jackie turned down one of her ideas for the pub quiz for a start."

"Wasn't there something about their Paul taking money out of the till?"

Gran gave her an old-fashioned look. "Trust a copper to remember that. It was never proven. The books were clean. Did you only get two pieces of pineapple upside-down cake?"

"Yes, but if you're good I'll take you to lunch at the café where I bought it the next time I get a day off. It's like the Flag but without the free-range wildlife."

Eithan glanced at her quizzically. Dee replayed what she'd just said. Oh God, she was starting to talk like the guvnor.

"Today," said Gran.

"What about today?"

"Today would do nicely. I was going to birthday bingo and a bit of lunch with Kay Diamond, but she's in for a hip replacement. Bumped up the waiting list on account of making a fuss on the telly. Did you see her? She had her hair done special. It was that reporter who's retired now who came. She said he was ever so nice. Had a cup of tea and everything. The cameraman ate all the biscuits, but they were the funny ones she won in the Easter raffle so it didn't matter."

"I'm hungry," said Tessa who'd arranged all the birthday cards on the table and was showing signs of boredom.

Dee looked at Eithan. He made a resigned face. "Might as well as there's no Taekwon Do."

She wrinkled her nose at him. "The food's good and over the road there's a common where the kids can race around and wear themselves out."

"Winner."

Dee returned her attention to Gran. "Get yourself ready, then, and never say I don't do anything for you. Violet Renshaw must have got on with someone here, surely?"

"Only Selma Peterson. When Selma died of a heart attack, Violet moved away. Can't say we miss her."

"Did she have family?"

"Who, Selma? Nephew in Australia. She was always whining about how he never wrote. He didn't come over for the funeral either. Not that it was much of one. Twenty minutes at the crematorium and not even a cup of tea afterwards. Skinflint stuff. I want a slap-up do when I go. I've told your mum." She looked at Eithan. "One of your ma's rum cakes too. That'll get them rolling in the aisles."

"Not Selma. Violet Renshaw."

Gran got to her feet. "Widow. Never mentioned kids. Like I say, she wasn't here long enough to get to know her. Only two or three years."

Dee made a note on her phone and forwarded it to the guvnor. *Sutton: trouble with Flag café (food inspectors) and the pub (till theft reported) when Violet lived here. Could run a check on deceased resident Selma Peterson. Friend of Violet. V moved after SP died. Gran doesn't know any next-of-kin.*

Annie was frowning intently at her canvas when her phone reverberated with a text alert.

"Damn," she said aloud. She usually turned it off in the studio. She reached to do it now, but her concentration had been broken. The painting was as finished as it was ever going to be anyway. She was only staring at it because she was putting off making a scary decision.

The text was from Calli, telling her to come to the library pronto with business cards. Heather Meadows had shown up looking for her and there had been developments.

Annie's heart thumped. Heather Meadows? It was difficult to suppress the tingle of hope that ran through her. *Hope doesn't put food on the table, Annie. Expect the worst and you won't be disappointed.* That was her grandmother's voice, rattling down through the years. *That's right, Grandma, keep me grounded.* She whistled for the dogs and set off. If Pat Williams could take Rupert, she didn't see why Sofi and Star shouldn't enjoy an outing to Calli's library as well.

She arrived at the same time as Gideon. The dogs wagged their tails happily.

"Hello," he said, "Did you get a summons too?"

"Developments, I was told. What sort of developments?"

"Only one way to find out."

Inside, a swift glance told Annie the reading group was noisily in possession of the first bay. "You might have warned me," she muttered to Calli.

Calli cast a wary glance at Minna Saxon, huddled in one of the deep chairs sniffling over a steaming mug. "Tell me about it. Never again. Listen, Heather Meadows came in on the way back from her book tour looking for your address. She'd given your card to her agent, who's in hospital having broken her leg and in no state to do business."

Heather hadn't been simply being polite! She did want her to illustrate the book! Annie felt a smile spread across her face. An extraordinary feeling of well-being suffused her. Lord, it felt weird. "Fantastic. Where is she?"

"Kenelm took her off to see Macready. Brace yourself. She's Violet's half-sister."

"You're joking."

Calli cast another glance at Minna and lowered

her voice to a murmur. "She's also Violet's beneficiary. Unfortunately, Minna thought that was her, so she went into meltdown. That's why the reading group are hanging on. They're hoping for an encore when Kenelm comes back for her."

"Poor Minna," said Gideon.

Calli nodded. "I'm liking Violet less and less with each new revelation."

Minna must have sensed they were talking about her. She raised a doleful face. "It's a mistake."

Calli crossed the room and squeezed her hand. "It doesn't sound it. I'm afraid it's true, Minna."

"It can't be. Heather's mixed her up with someone else. She said Violet wasn't kind, but she *was*. She really was."

"To you, maybe. Not always to others."

"How was she kind?" asked Gideon, pulling up a chair and beckoning Annie to bring the dogs over. "It'll help to talk about it."

Annie rolled her eyes at Calli. That was Gideon all over, taking minute pains over a little dab of a woman everyone else forgot. Still, Sofi and Star brought joy to Mum and the care home residents. It was worth a try.

Minna did seem calmer as she stroked Sofi. "Violet was kind in lots of ways," she said. "Giving me plants from her garden. Telling me about things I could claim for. Inviting me next door for proper coffee and nice biscuits and letting me watch *Strictly Come Dancing* and *Bake Off* on her lovely television. She's been kind right from the beginning. She even cooked Bombay duck for Father - and he didn't like her."

"Pardon?" said Gideon.

"Bombay duck, such a horrid smell, but Father loved it. You eat it with curry. I used to buy it for him from the *Curry in a Hurry* van, but Violet said it was much cheaper to cook it at home and it would save me walking along to Church Lea and standing in the queue, although that didn't used to worry me because it was somewhere to go and there are always people to talk to. She was so kind. She made it in her house and then brought it across because she didn't have much sense of smell, so it didn't bother her. And she fed Timmy fishy in the mornings because I couldn't afford it and she said it would be our little secret about me borrowing a few coins from her pot of change. She never shouted about it and locked me in like Father used to. That was kind too."

Annie saw Calli's lips tighten and felt her own blood pressure start to rise. It sounded like the same sort of 'kind' that Oscar had been. Laughingly taking charge of the cheque book when Annie was at art school so Mum wouldn't need to muddle her beautiful head with money. Considerately staying away at weekends so they could have lovely mother-daughter time together. Telling her he would always look after her. Another word for it was manipulative.

"Well," said Calli, "you explain all that to Inspector Gray. Have you finished your tea? Here he is now to take you to see Mr Macready again."

The dogs were ecstatic to see Kenelm. This was turning into their best day ever. He bent automatically to stroke them, on duty though he was. Annie was surprised to find warmth welling up in her. He wouldn't have done that a fortnight ago.

Minna went with Kenelm as docile as a lamb. With her departure, the reading group decided there was no point prolonging the meeting.

"Thank goodness for that," said Calli after she'd ushered them out. "As soon as Heather gets back from her grilling, I'll lock up. Keep an eye out for her while I stack all these mugs in the dishwasher. Glory, what a morning."

"Goodness, what a morning," echoed Heather a little later. "Are you sure you didn't mind me coming back? I can't tell you how pleased I am to have located you, Annie."

Me too. Annie smiled noncommittally, trying not to look needy.

"Don't give it another thought," said Calli. "We're dying to hear about you being Violet's half-sister. We had no idea."

Heather made a comical face of resignation. "That was how she preferred it. She was really very unlikeable. I saw her as little as possible. That's why I came to the library to find you, Annie, rather than asking her. If she'd known I was interested, she'd have disclaimed all knowledge of you, purely to spite me."

"Why?" asked Annie. To her at this moment, Heather seemed too good to be true. She might as well find out the downside. It wouldn't stop her signing a contract, but at least she'd be forewarned.

"She hated me. Our father married twice. Unhappy first marriage produced Violet. Happy second one produced me. Violet idolised Dad and took his departure very hard. He stayed on amicable terms with them because he was the loveliest man and he felt guilty about escaping. Personally, I'm not surprised he left her mother for mine. Anyone would. She was a dreadful, bitter, grasping woman. He said he was tricked into the marriage."

Annie snorted. "That figures. Violet had to get her pretty ways from someone."

"Violet was six years older than me and terribly hard work. When we were children she was eaten up with jealousy because Dad lived with us, not with her. She was quite vicious behind the grown-ups' backs until she realised she would see more of him if she pretended to be fond of me. I wasn't fooled. Children aren't, are they? She never left off being jealous. She stalked my social media feeds and was furious when one of my friends let slip online about the TV possibility. She rang me up straight away to carp that I hadn't told her."

"She liked to know things first?" asked Calli.

"That too - although if I had told her, she'd have thought I was boasting - but mostly she resented my success. Really resented it."

"Ah, I see. It still seems odd that she never mentioned a sister."

"To her I was an interloper, not a sister. However, she liked the glamour of being important, the sort of person who knows useful people, which I was on occasion. She had a desperate need to be admired. I assume that's why she kept moving from place to place after her husband died. She was always looking for a new group to be the centre of." She shrugged. "The trouble was, people gradually found out her real nature and her popularity waned as a result. Even then she might have stayed in her first house if her closest friend hadn't fallen ill and slipped away. Violet said the town held too many sad memories after that, so she was going to make a fresh start."

"I can understand that," said Calli.

"Oh yes, me too, but she milked it so. I would have helped her settle in to the new place, but she refused, saying she must 'learn to be independent' in such a brave voice I wanted to slap her. She claimed she never told anyone about our relationship because then she couldn't recommend me for talks. Really, it was because she wanted people to be impressed by her distinguished connections in the publishing world. As if I needed her to recommend me anyway! My agent organises plenty of gigs and I've been established on the WI circuit for years."

"Why did you pander to her then?" asked Annie. "I wouldn't have done."

Heather's hand rose and fell. "Inherited guilt, I suppose.

This talk was a prime example, squeezing it in for her as a favour on the eve of my book tour - which she knew full well about - simply because she said it had to be that day. One is always nicer to people one dislikes, don't you think?"

"No," said Annie.

"Heather is talking about normal people," said Gideon.

Annie made a face at him and bent to give Star a rub. Sofi, she noticed guiltily, was stretched out under the table, blissfully shedding golden hairs all over Calli's carpet.

"Did she take up gardening and produce those terrible pamphlets to imitate you?" asked Calli.

Heather nodded ruefully. "I think so, yes. Aren't they appalling? Dad was an amateur botanist so we both had an early interest in the subject. I went on to study it at university, whereas she rootled around in folk lore and dubious herbologies.

"What really puzzles me is why she left everything to you, if she didn't like you?" said Gideon.

"Originally she left it to Dad, with a reversion to me. Playing the devoted daughter. Applying a guilt trip from beyond the grave. He and Mum were killed in a crash several years ago and she tells me every time I see her that she's never changed her will. Trying to make me feel beholden or embarrassed. It's not as if I need the money. She had horrendously expensive tastes, so I doubt there will be much left after the house has been paid off. Her last revenge, making me deal with it all. But there you go, I can't get out of it. She was Dad's daughter before he met Mum, after all. I'm sorry for that poor little woman Violet deceived. A lot of her special friends were lonely and gullible. It makes it worse, doesn't it? Would she be offended if I ask whether she'd like anything out of the house or the garden before I sell?"

"I think Minna would take that very kindly," said Calli. She looked at Annie.

Annie nodded. "For sure."

"Good," said Heather. "I'll make a note for my solicitor. Before I get embroiled in all that, can we go to your studio and talk illustrations, Annie? I refuse to let Violet derail my working life as well as my personal time."

Yes! "Walk this way," said Annie, getting up and clicking her fingers for the dogs. "Come on, hounds. Home time." *I might even break out the extra-special dog treats for you in celebration.*

CHAPTER EIGHTEEN

As the door closed behind Heather Meadows, Detective Superintendent Macready eyed Kenelm sourly. "I asked you to find the deceased's next-of-kin, Inspector. I did not ask you to find me another suspect with a motive for bumping her off, complete with means and opportunity."

Don't rise to him. Better that he works off his bad temper on me than on the village. "From the reports of the meeting in the church hall, it doesn't seem possible Ms Meadows could have introduced the hemlock there," said Kenelm, trying to ignore the way he was starting to think like Gideon. "The tubs of food were left on a communal table. People helped themselves."

"Nothing to stop her slipping her sister a doctored cream cake to take home in her handbag for later. I'll detail someone to look at her finances. Let's have the neighbour in, then I'm off to some junkie that's got himself topped. God, it's a wonderful life. Follow up Ms Meadows's solicitor, assuming he isn't also on a climbing holiday. After that, you can release this place."

"Right, sir. What about the church hall?"

"Yes, yes, release that too." He made an irritable swatting motion with his hand. "Get the neighbour. I haven't got all day."

Kenelm left a message for his mother that the church coffee rota could proceed tomorrow unhindered by the presence of the law, saw Minna back next door after her interview, sealed the bungalow for hopefully the last time and returned to Hope Cottage to grab a bite to eat. Coming through the side gate, he saw figures moving across the wide windows of Annie's studio. In the kitchen his attention was caught by the sound of voices.

Sofi padded out of the studio to meet him, her tail thumping the door further open. Glancing in, Kenelm experienced a profound shock. Annie was talking animatedly to Heather Meadows. Her movements were quick and sure, she was vivid and properly filled-out, with a driving inner certainty that he'd never seen in her before. Her sheer vitality was a revelation.

He turned aside, clattering the kettle and the toaster to let her know he was back. She was a different woman, transformed. Because she was discussing her work with someone who understood it? Or because Heather had promised her a contract, alleviating her worries about money for the care home fees for a while? Whichever it was, she wouldn't want him to have glimpsed that vulnerability. He leaned against the worktop and was deep in his texts when they both came out together. *Focus on your work, Kenelm. Safest way to not say anything stupid.*

"Your toast is burning," said Annie, putting two mugs in the sink.

"Hell. Thanks." He buttered it quickly, pondering Dee's text regarding Sutton. "Why did Violet move from her last house?" he asked Heather.

She made a deprecating gesture. "Why did she ever move? I daresay it was because the neighbours weren't full of enough praise and glory. She was like that, constantly needing to 'be someone'. She loved being adored. It validated her. I was telling your friends about her earlier.

If it's of any interest, I'm sure she was thinking of moving away from here soon. She always asks me to do a talk as a sort of final flourish, so people remember her as important. She never stays - stayed - anywhere for long."

"That's interesting. The police team came to the same conclusion based on her internet searches and recent taxi journeys. You don't know of anyone in particular who disliked her?"

"Apart from me? No, sorry." She made a face. "Oh dear, in the deliciousness of talking book illustrations with Annie, I'd almost forgotten how much I have to do. Wretched, tedious woman. I'd better get back home and find you the solicitor's details and that list of the samples I prepared for the talk. Who do I ask whether one of my food containers has been absorbed into the church hall stock, do you know? Violet busily piled everything into the car at the end of my talk, so I didn't realise one was missing until I got home."

"That would be the vicar, once the hall has been released."

"Thank you. I'll be in touch, Annie."

As she drove off, Annie gave him a sideways glance. "If you arrest her for doing Violet in, I am never speaking to you again."

"And there was me thinking her appearance on the scene would take the heat off you. Can I still lodge here even if you're not speaking to me?"

"Hell yes, I'll need the money even more if I don't get Heather's contract. You're not serious, Kenelm?"

"Means, knowledge, opportunity, motive. Macready's very tempted, apart from the minor circumstance of all the hatred apparently being on the other side of the relationship. That and the lack of hard evidence."

"What are you doing eating toast, then? Get out there and find someone else for him to fancy. Jerry Ellwood for preference, no one will shed any tears for him, apart from possibly Bonita. Heather says she doesn't need the money, by the way."

"Go ask a detective. All I do is actions. And whatever Heather Meadows says, people always need money." His phone rang. He looked at the display. "I don't believe this. It's Sarah. I am never going to be able to write up my notes."

Annie screwed up her face in sympathy. "I'll put the kettle back on."

"Cheers. Hi Sarah, what is it? I'm working."

His wife's voice was petulant. "You're always working. It's Saturday, for God's sake, and don't give me that crap about crime happening 24/7, because I've heard it all before. Why don't you ever do anything useful like catching the bastards who set fire to the leisure centre?"

Kenelm bit his tongue on all the responses he could have made to this. "Word is an arrest is in sight. What's the problem, Sarah?"

Her voice rose. "I'm at the end of my tether is what the problem is. I'm the one on the go all day every day, not you or your bloody criminals. Now the boys' swimming gala tomorrow has been cancelled because they've decided the whole leisure centre roof might be unsafe even though the fire was at the other end. Just when I'd made arrangements to see Gail and have a few hours to myself for a change. Why can't they take the damn roof off and let them swim in the open air? That's how I learnt when I was a kid. What the hell am I supposed to do with the pair of them now? I just..."

"They can come to me. I'll have them for the whole day," he broke in, sick of her martyrdom. "That's what you wanted, isn't it? Next time ask straight off instead of beating about the bush. I will pick them up at ten tomorrow and drop them back at five. We can have Sunday lunch with their grandparents at the Manor - who will be delighted - then have a kickabout on the common." He stopped, hearing himself, hearing her, hearing echoes of the many, many arguments they'd had this past year. Also, paradoxically, hearing himself suggesting to Annie that maybe her grandma had been too busy with life to remember about having fun. And seeing a newly-vibrant Annie with the weight of anxiety lifted off her for a moment.

He cleared his throat. "You never need to worry about asking, Sarah," he said, making an effort to fetch up a conciliatory tone from amongst a wasteland of recriminations. "I know I work all hours, but I can manage to invent time if I need to. It's important for you to have a proper break now and again. Tell the boys to bring a football and clothes that don't mind getting muddy. See you tomorrow." He finished the call before he ruined it and rang his mother to warn her of augmented numbers for Sunday lunch with the first, faint feeling of being ahead of the game.

"This is nice and busy," said Gran approvingly as Dee pushed open the door of the *Cosy Kettle*. "I never trust cafés that are half empty. Makes you wonder why."

"It's always busy. That's why I rang first to make sure there would be space."

"Table at the far end. You've got a couple of friends down there," called Bessie. She nodded brightly at Gran. "Happy birthday."

Dee experienced a twinge of alarm. Friends? Not the guvnor, surely? But as they wove between tables heading for the empty one, a fair-haired woman looked up and did a double take.

"Hello," said Suzy Emmet. "I nearly didn't recognise

you in ordinary clothes. Don't you look nice! Are these your twins?"

"Trust me, I wouldn't be bringing them out for lunch if they weren't. This one's Tessa, that's Billy, my husband is Eithan and this is my gran. It's her birthday."

"Happy birthday! This is my Shannon and my Harry. You've already met Mrs C. We're having another treat. Mrs C likes treats."

"Not much left except treats when you get to my age, and I don't see why you should cook for me all the time," said Mrs Candour. She smiled in an interested fashion at Dee's gran. "Many happy returns. It's nice to have family to take you out. If any of mine ever get around to visiting, I have to take them."

"Fat chance of that with Gran, is there?" said Dee. "Don't let the size of Eithan fool you, by the way. He's the original gentle giant, softer than cheap marge."

He smiled at her lazily and reached for the menu.

"Causes him no end of trouble," she continued. "There's always an idiot drunk at the pub who won't believe someone his size isn't spoiling for a fight and is willing to have a go."

"Preach," said Suzy. "Wayne would have been first in line. I can't believe how free I feel now."

Suzy's son was regarding the twins with undisguised speculation. "D'you play football? We're going on the common after, but Mum's useless. I've got a ball with me."

"Awesome," said Tessa and Billy in unison. "Can we, Dad?"

"There is a god," murmured Eithan. "I love this village already."

Suzy grinned at Dee. "Might as well push these tables together. It'll be easier for the kids to get to know each other. Bessie won't mind."

"Course I don't," said the proprietor, arriving with her

notepad. She eyed Eithan thoughtfully. "That Jamaican black rum cake you mentioned," she said to Dee. "I was telling my Nancy about it and she wondered if your ma-in-law might part with the recipe?"

"Sure," said Eithan. "She starts soaking the fruit about three months before Christmas, mind. Me and my brother used to take turns stealing a spoonful after school. We took no end of trouble not getting caught. It never occurred to us that the level in the jar stayed the same."

Mrs Candour chuckled. "You missed all the fun this morning," she said to Dee. "The WI speaker was in the library looking for Annie Dearlove. Turns out she's Violet's half sister. The state of poor Minna Saxon! She had no idea. I felt so sorry for her."

That would please the guvnor. Another thing off his list. Meanwhile the twins were getting on well with Suzy's two which meant, if they properly wore themselves out, she and Eithan might actually get some time to themselves this evening.

CHAPTER NINETEEN

Kenelm had finished his report and added Dee's observations regarding Violet's previous sojourn in Sutton to the case records when his phone rang.

"Inspector Gray? The officer dealing with the late Mrs Violet Renshaw?"

"Speaking," replied Kenelm, wondering what was coming next. The voice was brisk and businesslike, but he wouldn't put it past a reporter on the local press to have somehow got hold of his number.

"Good afternoon. My name is Lucia Harbottle. My client Heather Meadows has informed me of her half-sister's demise. I understand you would like confirmation that we hold Mrs Renshaw's last will and testament."

Wonders would never cease. "If you are her solicitor, then I would indeed."

"I am authorised to email you a scan of the document. In layman's terms, she left everything to Mrs Heather Meadows, so it will be quite in order for you to release the late Mrs Renshaw's property to my client. May I ask if you have formed an opinion as to cause of death?"

"It was poison, whether accidental or deliberate we have yet to ascertain."

There was a pause from the other end of the phone.

"I see. How very unpleasant. If you let me have a secure address I will send the email."

Kenelm dictated it, then said, "It has been suggested Mrs Renshaw was considering moving. Did she consult you on that?"

The voice became a shade more frosty. "We dealt only with her will, Inspector. I understood her to use other firms for conveyancing."

While he waited for the email to come through, his phone buzzed with a text from Calli saying Gideon was making a giant vat of curry, so would he come and help eat it this evening? The text added that she was asking Annie as well.

Kenelm grunted cynically. The inference was obvious. They wanted to know how the case was progressing. However, home-cooked was home-cooked. He sent back an assent, left a message on Heather Meadows's phone to let her know she could pick up the keys to the bungalow on Monday and added a note to that effect to the file for Macready.

There was a knock on the door, followed by Annie with a pile of laundry. "I thought you might like clean bedding if the boys are coming over tomorrow."

"I doubt they'll notice."

"No, but they might video the room for their mother to see."

Sarah was unlikely to care one way or another, but it could save a gripe or two. "Thanks. That's thoughtful. Just leave it and I'll change the bed later." He got up and moved to the window, and was again pulled up short by the view. "It's weird, I keep expecting to see Church Lea like it used to be when I first went to Sunday school, which is daft because it hasn't been a green space for nearly forty years."

Annie joined him at the window. "Subconscious harking back to simpler days, perhaps?" She shook her head. "Brains *are* weird. Mum alternates between asking if it's time for the fete on the Lea yet and telling me stories of the builders treading mud across the road cadging cups of tea while Grandma was at work. She flits between time periods like Dr Who on speed."

"I'm sorry."

She shrugged. "Nothing we can do. Maybe you're picking up Grandma's memories of the Lea. This was her room. I've always felt awkward using it, that's why it was the first one I rented out when I started Airbnb. I thought it might cleanse the vibes. Grandma hated the new estate because it was modern and noisy and it spoiled her view of the church. She'd stand here glaring at the builders before she went off to catch the bus for work. Mum used to reckon she was ill-wishing them."

"And yet without the influx of young families, the school would have shut by now and half the shops on Church Parade and New Parade would have gone out of business."

"That's what Gideon says. He's all for progress as long as it keeps the village alive. You're both very practical." She hesitated, flushing. "Talking of being practical, I've taken your advice. I've blocked out the other rooms for a couple of weeks after next weekend. I suddenly wondered if I was making the Airbnb visitors an excuse for not giving Bunty a firm answer."

"Daring yourself to do it?"

"Something like that."

"You can blame me if it goes wrong." *Everybody else does.*

She shook her head seriously. "It wouldn't be a case of blaming anyone. I need to prove I can still work full-time on a painting without distractions. I used to be able to, but it's a long while since I didn't have to keep stopping to check up on Mum. I'm hoping the act of creation might clear my head of that guilt too. It's even worse now I know Violet sent the Oscar postcard to get even with *me*, not with Mum. It means Mum is suffering because I couldn't keep a reign on my tongue."

"She'd have found another grudge to pay back. Once she'd decided to send the postcard, any excuse would do. Did you see Calli and Gideon have invited us over for curry this evening?"

"Gideon is such a pain. He will keep trying to rehabilitate me with enforced socialising. He's always been the same, right from when I was the illegitimate kid that everyone whispered about behind my back. This is my friend Annie, he'd say. You *will* be nice to her."

He grinned. "I think this time they mostly want to know about the case."

"I accepted anyway. Pointless not to. Besides, tonight's visitors are four girls going to a big party at Woodberry Court. I just know they're going to be screeching and drinking cheap wine and doing each other's make up for hours."

Kenelm grimaced. "We'll go to Calli's early." He darted a look at her. "I asked Gideon about making a desk and shelving unit for the end wall in here. Something that would be in keeping with the cottage. Do you mind?"

She raised her eyebrows. "You'll pay for a beautiful hand-crafted desk for a room I've never felt was mine and you're concerned I might mind? You worry about the craziest things."

Kenelm's phone buzzed. "Confirmation of the will. Good. I'll take the church hall keys back to the rectory, then unseal Riverdene and give it a last once-over before I head to Ely for what's left of my shift. Is it just me or has today lasted for about a fortnight already?"

"I have that feeling all the time and I'm still always stumbling around trying to catch up."

He grunted in sympathy. "Hopefully, being able to paint for longer will help. See you later."

The bungalow was empty of life. Even Violet Renshaw's overpowering scent had faded. Kenelm wondered how many of the forensics team had been given a hard time by their partners over the lingering smell on their clothes. He glanced around, not envying Heather Meadows the job of clearing out all the knick-knacks and frilly furniture before selling. He went into the back garden to check the gate was secure, thinking how much nicer Annie's haphazard, crowded cottage-garden was to this rigid gaiety. Across the fence, the usual game of football was taking place on the common. The players were a bit young for Tom and Rick, but maybe it didn't matter where sport was concerned. There were a couple of teenagers watching. They might want to join in a game with his boys tomorrow. He reflected wryly that he must be settling into the village because some of the parents keeping an eye on their offspring looked familiar. He narrowed his eyes. One of them especially. And she wasn't from Fencross Parva.

As if aware of the scrutiny, the compact woman in jeans and a red sweater turned around, clocked him and jogged up to the fence. "Afternoon, guvnor."

"Revising your opinion of Fencross Parva, Bryce?"

"Nice to see you too, sir. We were conned into bringing Gran for a birthday lunch at the *Cosy Kettle* due to the leisure centre being out of action. She's still in the café with Topsy Candour, ordering pots of tea like there's a whole string of loos between here and Sutton. We're trying to wear the kids out." She nodded at the garden behind him. "Fancy, isn't it? Gran says Violet brought half the plants from her old garden with her. The buyers were furious. It was only a small terraced place she had there, nothing special. The garden was the best bit of it."

Kenelm gave a cynical grunt. "She'd probably have done the same here too. Heather Meadows is sure Violet was about to move. Did you get my text about her being Violet's half-sister?"

"Yup. Bessie at the café knew all about it too."

"You amaze me." He contemplated the pond area where Annie's boot prints had given him such a disagreeable shock that first day. His gaze travelled over the pond, over the scrubby, fragrant herbs, and got caught on the same sense of dissatisfaction he'd experienced before. Why was the fence area so untidy? It was out of character. Almost without realising, he focused on the low greenery, on the crinkle-edged leaves against the fence. And then he reached for his phone, swearing long and hard.

"What's up?" asked Dee.

"Over there. Look over bloody there." And into the phone, "Annie, can you come to Riverdene? I'm in the back garden."

Anne came the short way, across the corner of the common. She nodded at Dee, then scowled over the fence. "Now what?" she asked. "I thought you were going to Ely."

Kenelm let her through the gate. "I was. I may still be. Look carefully at this garden and tell me what you see."

"This garden that your forensic team searched?"

"This garden that the senior investigative officer's forensic team *should* have searched. That's why I need an independent opinion."

"Any particular area? Only I am quite busy."

"The wild patch by the pond."

Annie snorted. "That's not wild. Everything has been carefully planted. There's nothing wild about it at all."

"Humour me."

A minute later, with Annie's impressive curses turning the air blue, he was on the phone to Detective Superintendent Macready.

For once, there was utter silence after he delivered his short statement. He considerately switched it to loudspeaker so Dee could enjoy it. "Repeat that, Inspector?" said Macready at last. "For a moment I thought you said you've identified hemlock in the late Violet Renshaw's garden."

His dangerous, clipped tone matched Kenelm's sentiments exactly. *This* garden, of all the places in Fencross Parva, to find it. "Affirmative, sir. I have independent confirmation."

"I'll be there in twenty minutes."

Kenelm put his phone away. Detective Superintendent Macready's language beat his and Annie's put together.

Dee's husband loped across from the football game. "Can't leave you alone for a moment," he said to her. He nodded in a friendly fashion at Kenelm. "Car still going okay?"

"Hasn't given me a moment's trouble since you fixed it."

"The guvnor's found hemlock in the dead woman's garden," said Dee.

Eithan shook his head sorrowfully. "And there was I thinking it was such a nice village."

They were interrupted by Annie hurrying back, complete with sketchbook.

"What the blue blazes are you up to?" Kenelm asked.

"Drawing the hemlock in situ before we dig it up and destroy it. It's exactly the sort of thing Heather wants for her new book. I won't get in anyone's way."

Behind Eithan, the footballers and onlookers had wandered over to see what was going on.

"Dad, you're not watching us. I nearly scored then."

"Sure I am, Tess. You were robbed."

"Hemlock?" shrieked Suzy, having overheard Annie. "She had it in her own garden all along? Mrs C *said* she was useless. You're not going to close the common again, are you? Not on a weekend? The village will go mental."

Dee's son's eyes widened enviously. "Do you come here every day?" he said to Suzy's youngest. "You're well lucky having all this space across the road. Wish we did. We've only got a titchy garden."

"We've only got a titchy house," pointed out Eithan.

"This one will be for sale soon," said Kenelm blandly. "You could move to Fencross Parva."

"Can't afford it," replied Dee, glaring daggers at him.

Eithan gaze travelled thoughtfully over the bungalow. "We could. This won't fetch much, but it wouldn't be big enough. Two bedrooms, isn't it? We'd have to put in a loft conversion. Or we could add an extension at the back. Big garden. Enough space for a workshop."

Dee put her hands on her hips. "Eithan Bryce, do I look like the sort of person who lives on a road called Mulberry Lane?"

He smiled happily at her. "Know what there isn't in this village?"

"Let me see. A cinema? Swimming baths? Toyshop? Useful relatives to have the kids after school when both of us are working?"

"A garage, babe. There isn't a garage."

Dee gave a faint moan. "Eithan, you cannot open your own garage between two residential houses."

"There are the derelict stables at the end of the road," said Kenelm, enjoying himself immensely. "Plenty of space for a garage there. Massive customer base. You'd easily get planning permission, they're a terrible eyesore as they are."

Eithan looked interested. "Who owns them?"

Dee made a show of checking her watch. "Come on, you lot. Gran will think we've been mugged. We'll come over another weekend, Suzy. I'll text you and fix something up."

"Leaving so soon?" asked Kenelm.

She threw him a dirty look. "I don't want you giving my fella any more ideas about moving. They're already starting to think of us as regulars at the café and they've only just met him and the kids."

"But think how relieved Minna Saxon would be to have a fine, upstanding young family at the end of the road instead of tramps and vagabonds."

"Give my regards to Mr Macready, sir. See you next week."

Kenelm watched the group head towards the exit from the common. Aside from the pleasure of winding Dee up, his mind was buzzing with speculation. Things they'd said had got him thinking. If Violet hadn't made a large profit on her previous house sale - and it didn't sound as though a small, 'nothing special' terrace would provide one - then where had the hefty bank account increase come from that she'd been spending for the last few years? If Eithan was right and she'd been unlikely to make a profit on Riverdene either, then what was she planning to live on when she relocated again?

CHAPTER TWENTY

Annie sketched hard and fast, and didn't hear Kenelm until he'd repeated his question.

"I said, will you have finished by the time Macready gets here?"

"Yes. When's he coming?"

"Twenty minutes is what he said. But that was ten minutes ago."

"Good, I can make a quick wash painting too." She turned the page with one hand and felt in her smock with the other for her painting tin and water bottle.

"Do you always travel around with the contents of an art shop?" he asked after a moment or two.

"Tools of the trade, like you always having your police radio with you, even when you're off duty. This is my pocket kit. I've got more in the satchel. I'll be quicker if I'm not interrupted."

"Hint taken. Sorry."

"You can talk as long as you're okay with not getting an answer." She caught up with what she was saying and was so surprised she had to pause, brush poised, before she laid down another leaf. There were very few people she could tolerate watching her work. Why was Kenelm suddenly one of them? *Because he doesn't intrude. He simply accepts it as what I do.*

"Thanks, but I'd be better off making notes for my report."

Annie concentrated on the hemlock, watching it grow on the page. Violet had to have known this was here. It hadn't appeared by itself. Around it were other herbs. Rosemary, sage and mint sunk in pots, a straggly scramble of thyme.

"This was deliberate," she said aloud. "If Violet had really thought it was parsley, it would have been planted at the front, not concealed behind a stand of lavender."

"I'll tell Macready," he said, sounding abstracted, and broke off as a car stopped outside with a squeal of brakes. "That will be him now. Can you finish up? Then hang around to be an expert witness, if you would?"

He went inside. Annie closed her tin and stashed everything back in her smock pocket, giving the painting a few more seconds to dry. Kenelm, bless him, was keeping the superintendent talking, presumably making his report. She got out her phone and took a rapid photo of the whole bed to send to Gideon.

Behind her on the common, more people than usual were walking dogs in this direction. Suzy would have been bound to mention the hemlock in the café when she went back for Topsy. The news would be all over Fencross Parva in half an hour. Less, probably.

The back door opened. Superintendent Macready stomped down the path and scowled at the pond. He was followed by two plain-clothes men. "That's it, is it?" he said.

"Over by the fence, yes," replied Kenelm. "As soon as I realised, I contacted Ms Dearlove to verify it."

The heavy stare was redirected to her. "You had an argument with the deceased the evening she died. Did you know the hemlock plant was here?"

"No," said Annie. "The only time I've been in this

garden was when the dogs escaped, and it was dark then."

"What are these other things?" He pointed to the nearby shrubs.

"Lavender, sage, mint, chives, rosemary..."

"All herbs."

"In this part by the pond, yes."

Macready conferred in a mutter with the plain-clothes men. Next door, Minna opened her back door with an apologetic, "Well, my garden is nothing like dear Violet's, of course, but if you really want to see it..."

Annie gave a grim smile. Her estimate of half an hour had been generous. Here was Bonita Ellwood already, sharp nose twitching, avid to see what was going on in Violet's garden now.

"Oh, hello dear," said Minna over the fence to Annie. "Bonita just called around with a slice of pie they couldn't finish and to check how I was after this morning's upset. Wasn't that kind of her?"

"Very thoughtful," said Annie, looking at the sliver of pastry on a paper plate that wouldn't have provided a malnourished chihuahua with a square meal.

"Easy to see what happened," said Macready to his subordinates. "The deceased snipped a couple of leaves and added it to her supper by mistake. Get a photo, Gray, then dig it up and put it in an evidence bag."

"Shouldn't forensics do it?"

"Forensics are booked solid for a week and you're the one with the key to the garden shed."

"You'll need protective gloves," said Annie. "I've got some if there are none here."

"I take it I'm insured?" asked Kenelm.

"Yes, you're bloody insured. Bag it, label it, bring it to the station. I've got three more cases I'm investigating. I'll be glad to finally sign this one off."

They hurried away. Kenelm stared after them with

compressed lips, looking exactly like Gideon when someone hadn't lived up to his expectations.

Next door, Bonita was welded to the fence. "Fancy. In her own garden all along. Is that it? Is that what killed her?"

Kenelm addressed her icily. "Mrs Renshaw died from ingesting hemlock leaves. This is hemlock. The appropriate tests will need to be carried out. Good afternoon to you."

"Really. Manners." Bonita flounced indoors, followed by Minna.

"Good riddance," muttered Kenelm. He got Violet's bunch of keys out of his pocket and eyed it trenchantly.

Annie sighed. "You want me to dig it out?" she asked. "Be a shame to mess up that nice uniform."

"Do you mind? It'll be quicker. I want to get it to the station and find out if anything came from the enquiries into her previous addresses. Dee gave me some interesting info that needs feeding in, assuming the case is still open. Bloody Macready. I know there's more to it than carelessness, but will he listen?"

"Doubt it. That was a man with his mind made up. We can talk it over with Gideon and Calli. You aren't going to be at peace until this is solved."

"You're confusing me with my cousin."

Annie gave a short laugh. "You have more in common with Gideon than either of you is willing to admit. Unlock the shed. I want to get the hemlock out of the ground as fast as you do."

"All I'm saying..." Bonita's voice came clearly to Calli as she opened the door of the shop. "All I'm saying is it's an odd thing for a woman who knew so much about plants to have poisoned herself by mistake."

Calli grimaced and moved swiftly to the far aisle to find a packet of rice before anyone saw her.

"*Supposed* to have known so much," said Rhona Lee. "Annie Dearlove would disagree. Personally, I never thought she was as good as she claimed."

"We all know you didn't like Violet."

"I won't miss her, that's for sure," said Rhona. "Not like poor Minna."

Calli found the rice, grabbed a pack of poppadums as well and headed for the counter in time to see Bonita's malicious smile.

"Yes, poor Minna," said Bonita. "After expecting to inherit everything too. She'll miss not popping next door via Violet's back garden every day."

They fell silent as Calli paid. Calli felt their eyes on her all the way out.

Bonita was talking again even before the shop door closed. "I told you where the hemlock was growing, didn't I? Barely a step or two from the path..."

"Not good," said Gideon, tending to a pan of spitting onion and spices as she relayed the conversation. "Next thing you know it will be all over the village that Minna did away with Violet for her house and savings. We'll have to do something to stop the talk."

"Like?"

"Finding the real killer would help. It's a puzzle, though. Annie sent me a photo of the garden. Have a look. She says the hemlock was deliberately planted behind the other herbs. Violet had to have known it was there."

Calli tapped open Gideon's phone and studied the photo. "I see what she means. It doesn't make sense. I suppose Violet *did* show lots of people around her garden. Other people may have spotted it and kept quiet." She looked across at him, enveloped in steam and a large barbeque apron. "Do you need me to do anything or shall I collect all our information together and lay it out on the table?"

He turned and grinned. "That's my girl. We can present Kenelm with the solution along with the meal."

The curry, however, had barely been put in the oven when the kitchen door opened to reveal Kenelm and Annie.

"You're early," said Gideon. "It'll be another hour at least yet."

"Sorry. Annie's visitors are shouting to each other between the rooms while they get ready for a party. They've already used all the hot water and downed two bottles of prosecco. I couldn't stand it any more so we smuggled out a bottle of shiraz before they found that too, and came straight over."

"God knows what state they'll be in when they get home," said Annie. "I can see I'm going to spend tomorrow morning scrubbing out the bathroom." She took a quick breath. "I'm going to close the bookings while I work on Bunty's painting. It was Kenelm's idea."

Oh, well done, Annie! Maybe that would lift the strain from her face. Calli got out glasses for them all and checked to see whether the wine was the sort that needed a corkscrew. You could never tell with Kenelm. "Two things to celebrate then. You getting some time to paint and Kenelm finding the hemlock."

Kenelm looked sardonic. "I don't think I'm in line for any plaudits for that. Macready is furious with the search team for not spotting it earlier. He is now even more convinced Violet was a bungling amateur who mistook hemlock for parsley and added it to her own supper. Accidental death due to incompetence. He's dialled hard back on any other enquiries."

"She didn't though," said Annie. "Mum might be away with the fairies half the time, but she says Violet wasn't stupid. She knew exactly what she was doing with that deadly nightshade, for example."

Calli exchanged a glance with Gideon. "We don't think so either. Bonita is already hinting Minna did it."

"Her," said Annie sourly. "As soon as the police cars turned up, she arrived next door with the smallest piece of left-over pie she could bring herself to part with that she thought Minna might like for her tea and then powered her way into the garden to see what was going on. There's no way a verdict of accidental death is going to stop her gossiping about it. It's going to be pretty rotten for Minna. It's no fun having people fall silent whenever you come into the room. It's one reason I stopped taking Mum to the WI meetings."

Gideon's lips tightened. "We need to sort it out. Calli's list of suspects is on the table along with the other info."

Kenelm reached across and picked it up. "My mother cut the piece of green cake. Pat Williams prodded the green cake, covering her action by asking about ingredients, knowing Violet would take the largest slice. She was also very quick to clear up afterwards."

"No, she only cleared up Heather's samples," said Calli. "Somebody else dealt with the cake plates. And why would it be her, anyway? She didn't know Violet had falsely reported her to the RSPCA."

"Unless Violet asked her how she'd got on, in that sweetly reasonable tone of hers," pointed out Annie. "That would give it away. Come to that, I might have lied about the argument that night in Violet's garden. I might have a secret store of hemlock and taken her a laced cheese straw as a fake olive branch."

"I've tasted your pastry," said Gideon. "Even Violet couldn't have been that greedy."

Kenelm continued to read the list aloud. "Bonita elbowed people aside to get to the green cake. She could have sprinkled hemlock on Violet's piece in revenge for Jerry being seen there again."

"Not without gloves on," objected Annie.

"Then there's still Heather Meadows. She might have lied about not needing the money. She could have given her something to eat."

"As could any number of her victims," said Calli. "The problem is there are too many suspects." She pulled another sheet of paper out of the pile. "Did Macready get anywhere with the list of ticks?"

Kenelm shook his head. "He hasn't mentioned it. It's possible he turned it over to his team. No one has checked with me to see if I know the people. Once he'd discounted regular blackmail payments, he lost interest."

"How did he make superintendent?" said Gideon.

"Speed, sarcasm, having the loudest voice and not looking beyond the obvious. There's even less reason to investigate her grudges and petty revenges now he's got the result he was after. Although, to be frank, I couldn't ever see him sending Dee and me out to knock on doors and ask what annoying thing happened to..." He glanced at the list and picked a name at random, "Desmond Saxon on June 15th five years ago."

"You wouldn't be able to anyway," answered Annie. "He's dead. He was Minna's father. Miserable so-and-so. Mum said he had the closed, bullying mind of a small-time insurance clerk right to the end. He used to run Minna ragged. Him dying was the best thing that ever happened to her, except she was then taken over by Violet."

"There's something in the other notebook about him shouting at Violet and being rude about her fence. That must be what the tick was in revenge for," said Calli. She frowned. "But in the library this morning, Minna said Violet was kind to him. That seems out of character."

Annie had paused with her glass of wine half-way to her lips. She looked at Gideon, then at Kenelm. "The tick was five years ago? He must have died about then. I know it was some time in the summer."

"Minna said Violet was kind because she used to cook Bombay duck for him," said Gideon slowly. "She had a poor sense of smell so the foul aroma didn't bother her."

"Was that why the bungalow was drenched in scent?" asked Kenelm. "So she could actually smell something?"

Annie shrugged. "Probably. I've never been inside."

"Trust me, it stank." There was a tiny silence, then Kenelm voiced what was in all their minds. "It does make you wonder if she cooked Bombay duck the day Desmond Saxon died. She *could* have added a little something extra to it. What was the cause of death?"

Annie shook her head. "I can't remember. Stroke maybe? Heart attack? He smoked and drank and took no exercise. The village had been expecting him to go for years."

"Was Dr Gotobed still practising?"

Calli thought back, remembering her tired, dedicated uncle. "Five years ago? Yes. He wanted to retire and was trying to sell the practice, but hadn't found a buyer and didn't want to leave the village without a GP so he carried on." She bit her lip unhappily. "He might have made a mistake about the cause, especially if he'd been expecting something of the sort."

Kenelm had the air of choosing his next words with deliberation. "Minna said when she found Violet *it was just like when Father went*. I'm beginning to wonder if she meant the expression on Violet's face, rather than the shock it gave her, finding the body."

"We could ask," said Gideon. "We could also ask if Violet had cooked Bombay duck for him the night before."

"You'll have to do it then. If I ask her officially, I'd have to record the answer. Suspecting Violet of bumping Desmond Saxon off, just to make her own life more comfortable, gives Minna an added motive for poisoning Violet. Vengeance as well as a nice bungalow to sell for her declining years."

"She couldn't," said Annie.

"Does Minna strike you as that clever?" said Gideon at the same time.

"Not remotely, but you'd be surprised what a copper sees."

Calli looked around her table, at her friends, her lover. How could they be so matter-of-fact about this? "We're suggesting Violet cold-bloodedly murdered her neighbour - her friend's father - as revenge because he was rude? That's horrible. It's really serious. That's not a petty repayment of a grudge. That's evil."

CHAPTER TWENTY-ONE

Annie stirred. In her eyes, Calli saw a bleak abhorrence. "I agree. The thing is, I *can* believe it of Violet, because she had no public conscience. She didn't care what havoc she caused. Her snide comments, all the little barbs she placed - she got a kick out of them. Murder would be just one step further on. What I *can't* believe is any of her targets retaliating in the same way. We know all these people, we've known them for years, we've lived alongside them. Its inconceivable that any of the names on that list would have killed Violet. None of them are nasty enough."

"And that," said Kenelm, "is why I'm the policeman, not you. I can believe anything of anyone. It might not have been retaliation. If Violet had nosed out a dangerous secret, putting her out of the way might seem the only option. Which brings me to another conundrum. Oh wait, before that, who owns the derelict stables at the end of Mulberry Lane?"

"Topsy Candour," said Gideon, mystified. "Her goddaughter had them years ago, but was diagnosed with cancer. The treatment wasn't as clever in those days. I don't think Topsy could bear to let them go. She's always said if there was a local willing to put in the time and money to build a useful business there, she'd consider leasing the land. She'd rather do that than have her family sell it to a developer for more executive houses. Why do you want to know?"

Unholy glee flitted across Kenelm's face. "Oh frabjous day. What if the person wasn't local, but was someone she liked and they relocated here with their family?"

"That would do it. Who?"

Kenelm smiled beatifically. "Dee's husband is an excellent mechanic. He wants his own garage. The stables would suit him perfectly. I cannot wait to see the appalled look on Dee's face when I tell him they could be available."

"You are a bad man," said Calli. "What's that got to do with your conundrum?"

"Just that they brought the twins over to play football with Suzy Emmet's kids on the common this afternoon. They were there when I found the hemlock and we got talking. Now, listen to this. Violet is supposed to have made money on each house move, then used those profits to live on until she moved again. She was planning another move shortly. But Dee's grandmother says she *didn't* make a lot of money from her house sale in Sutton last time. Eithan Bryce doubts she'd make a profit on Riverdene either."

"I'd agree with him," said Gideon. "So?"

"So where do her hefty lumps of cash come from when she moves? Dee told me the opinion in Sutton is that Violet left because a close friend of hers there had died. This is my point. We know she was incredibly nosy. Did she ferret out something about the death and was *paid* to move away? It fits with what we know of her character."

Calli sat bolt upright, looking at him in consternation. "What? A close friend died in *Sutton*? But Heather said Violet's best friend at her original house died! She thought that was why she sold up, because with her husband and her friend gone, the town had too many sad memories."

"That's quite the coincidence," murmured Gideon. He drummed his fingers thoughtfully on the table.

"She can't have found out about dodgy deaths every time," objected Annie. "She was planning to move again, but nobody's died here recently. Nobody has any big secret to be blackmailed with."

"That's why they are secrets," pointed out Kenelm. "It's in the definition."

Calli cudgelled her brain. Two deaths of friends had to mean something. It couldn't be just chance. She found she was staring at Gideon, seeing a reflection of her thought processes in his eyes. "Unless..."

Gideon nodded. "Just what I was thinking."

"What sort of close friend in Sutton, Kenelm? Similar to Minna?"

Kenelm looked at her blankly. "I have no idea. Why?"

"Do you know her name?" asked Gideon. "Can you look her up? Can you look up her will?"

"Her *will?*" said Kenelm, clearly wondering if they'd both lost their senses. "I don't see what you're getting at."

"Patterns," said Calli. A horrible, warped scheme was taking shape in her head. "That scene in the library with Minna. Suppose we've got this the wrong way around? You said Minna could have a motive because she was expecting Violet to leave everything to her. They made their wills together. Has anyone asked Minna what hers says? Did Violet persuade Minna to make a reciprocal bequest? Working backwards, what did the will of Violet's friend in Sutton say? What about her bestie in the original town? The one who died?"

Kenelm stared at her, then reached for his phone to log into his police account. "Give me a moment. Where's Dee when I need her? She's better at navigating this stuff than I am. Yes, all right, you can have a password, dammit. Estate of Selma Peterson. What do you mean you want another password? Bloody technology. Wait, here we go..." His eyes skimmed the text. "Bloody hell, you've nailed it, Calli."

"What?" said Gideon urgently. "What does it say?"

Kenelm looked up. "The late Selma Peterson left 'everything I die possessed of to my dear friend Violet Renshaw'. Exactly the same wording as on Violet's fake will."

"And that's what she's been living on?" said Annie into the silence. "Her best friend's money?"

"And the one before that and the one before that, maybe?" said Calli, feeling very sick. "I mean, it might have been coincidence. One of them may have been ill anyway. But it would be worth checking back to see whether her sudden influxes of money and subsequent house moves coincided with other dear pals' deaths."

"Heather did say Violet always chose the same sort of friend," said Annie. "Lonely, gullible women."

"I'm on it," said Kenelm, typing furiously on his phone. "I'm putting in a request."

"Patterns," said Gideon. "It works, Kenelm. Each move provides camouflage for an influx of money and fresh victims to set up the next."

"The next one in this case being Minna?" said Annie. "Targeting her for her house and her father's savings?"

Calli nodded. "I do really think so. Because as you said, the only person evil enough to have *planned* a useful accidental death for her friend was Violet herself. What an appalling woman. She must have been fuming when Covid and lockdown put all her plans on hold."

Gideon slammed his palm against his forehead. "Yes! Think about it. Violet's bungalow alone might not fetch much more than she paid for it, but the whole plot - hers and Minna's together - would be a really good sized area with the gardens added in. If a developer bought both and got planning permission, a clever architect could get a couple of five-bedroom houses with double garages in there. That would bring in more than enough for Violet to live on for the next few years."

"Can we prove it enough for the village to believe it and stop spreading insinuations about poor Minna?" asked Calli. "Day trips around the countryside and internet searches on two-bedroom houses in small villages aren't conclusive. Meriel does that sort of thing all the time with Georgian manors and architect-designed luxury apartments. It's how she relaxes. House porn, she calls it."

"Heather thought Violet was preparing to move," Kenelm reminded them. "I bet if pressed, Jerry Ellwood will say that when she summoned him for a valuation, she floated the rhetorical question of the amount both houses together would fetch as opposed to separately. Dee's report mentioned Violet had invited Minna to lunch the day after the WI meeting, the day she herself died. How much do you wager hemlock was on the menu?"

"And the beauty of it is she wouldn't get the blame," said Annie. "Minna is hard-up. She would be bound to sample everything at the talk. If she was taken ill within a day of the WI meeting, suspicion would naturally fall on Heather and her foraging recipes. This is the time of year when hemlock could conceivably be mistaken for parsley."

"It fits," said Calli. "We know from the notebooks Violet was mean, and we also know she was jealous of Heather. Younger sister, more attractive, more successful, her father's favourite. She probably thought it would serve her right to be accused of carelessness."

"She was lucky the talk was this month," said Annie. "Another few weeks and the hemlock would be tall and purple-spotted and stinky. No chance of hiding it in that garden. She'd have to keep cutting it down."

Calli shook her head. "Not lucky. Arranged. Heather said Violet was insistent she gave her talk this month. I'm feeling more and more sure of this."

Kenelm frowned. "Dee's notes indicated it was Heather who stipulated the date. That's what the WI secretary told her."

"You ask Heather. She fitted in the talk at great personal inconvenience."

"The WI secretary was doubtless told that by Violet," said Gideon. "I agree with Calli. This was well planned."

"Horrible woman," said Calli with a shudder. "If we are right, Minna is very lucky. I still don't see how Violet ate hemlock herself if she was planning to doctor lunch the *next* day. She knew what it was. Why on earth would she have even picked the wretched stuff a day early?"

Kenelm shrugged. "I don't know, but Pat Williams spotted her in her back garden on the morning of the WI talk weeding in latex gloves. That sounds a lot like skin protection. Maybe she intended to do it at the meeting before realising it wasn't possible."

"No," said Calli. "She would have known it wouldn't work. She's arranged talks by Heather before. She'd have seen Heather opening up the tubs as a free-for-all after the talk. She wasn't even *sitting* with Minna."

Kenelm gave a frustrated growl. "You're right. Minna told Macready that she hardly saw Violet at the meeting. She said she was busy the whole time. Unless Violet got it all ready for the next day's lunch beforehand for some reason, then absentmindedly forgot after she'd had her glass of wine and ate some."

Gideon nodded. "That's a possibility."

Calli wrinkled her nose, dissatisfied. She glanced at Annie to see what she made of the theory.

Annie's eyes were unfocused. Then she blinked suddenly. "She *could* have used the hemlock at the meeting, but not on Minna. Calli, we saw her. We saw Violet bring *Heather* a plate of salad after she finished her talk. Heather was more interested in talking about illustrations with me, so put it aside. We saw Pat empty that plate into one of those containers, untouched. We saw Violet smirk on the way back past my table. What if she was pleased because she thought Heather had eaten it? She hated Heather. She was jealous of her success and furious about the television contract. She could easily have added chopped hemlock to the plate before bringing it over, just to get rid of her. And it would add colour to bumping off Minna the following day. Two victims for the price of one."

Kenelm was staring at her in horror. "But the risk! What if Heather had seized up driving home and caused a multiple pile-up? For that matter *anyone* could have eaten it at the talk."

"Not necessarily," said Calli. "Or only Annie, and that wouldn't bother her one little bit. Similarly, if a traffic accident caused other deaths she'd write it off as collateral damage, the end justifying the means. I think you've solved it, Annie. Violet would have chopped the hemlock at home and put it in a polythene bag, so all she had to do was empty it on to the plate before bringing it across to Heather. Minna said Violet was giddy on the way back. She might have got some on her fingers shaking it out or throwing away the bag afterwards. Thank goodness Heather was busy with you and didn't eat the salad. Where did the left-overs go after Pat cleared up?"

"I expect she tipped the tub she was using into the bin. You could ring and ask her, Kenelm."

"Heather said she was missing a tub," said Kenelm. "She asked me about checking the church hall for it. Might it have got lumped in with the washing up?"

"Probably," said Annie. "The WI are fiends for washing up anything that doesn't move. The only objection I can see is that if Violet got hemlock on her fingers at the hall, I'd have thought it would affect her more quickly. She was fine and eating supper at eleven pm that night."

Calli looked at Kenelm. "Did the post-mortem say what she'd eaten?"

"Apart from hemlock? They found salad, quiche, cake

and wine in her stomach," said Kenelm. "The quiche in the fridge was clean, as was the open bottle of wine, but there was no salad so she must have finished that." He scrolled through his phone until he came to the video recording he'd made. "See for yourself."

"There's a space," said Calli, watching the video intently. "The fridge is packed full of food, but there is a clearly-square space on the top shelf. Heather's snaplock containers were square. Violet could have eaten the salad and thrown the container away."

"Circumstantial. There's another gap on the next shelf down," objected Gideon, leaning across to study it. "There, look."

"That'll be where Minna took the fish for the blasted cat," said Kenelm.

Minna. Minna! Oh dear God! Calli shot to her feet, rocking the table. "Christ, where's my phone list?"

Gideon got up too. "What is it?"

"Minna," she said, grabbed her phone and scrolling through the address book. *Please don't let it be too late.* "Don't you remember? Dee told us the only other new thing in Minna's fridge apart from the posh plates holding fish was a tub of salad. What if Violet greedily brought home the leftovers from the church hall, assuming Heather had eaten her plateful ages ago and the rest was all innocent? That would be how she came to have some of it for supper. But then, what if Minna took the remains from Violet's fridge at the same time as the fish? She thought everything was going to be hers. Violet might even have said they'd finish the salad for lunch the next day, meaning to add new, fresh hemlock to Minna's portion. And Minna had enjoyed Heather's samples and has been brought up to view waste as a sin." She raised the phone to her ear, willing Minna to answer.

Kenelm was sceptical. "What if she did? It didn't work.

She hasn't been ill. She was in the garden with Bonita when Annie and I found the plant."

"She hasn't been ill because of eating out on the strength of finding the body for the last two days. But the gossips all know about it now, so today she'll be at home nibbling on Bonita's bit of pie, potentially with left-over salad. Gideon, she's not answering."

He was already halfway out of the door. "If she does, tell her not to touch anything. You go ahead. I'll grab my tools in case the door's locked."

"In Fencross Parva?" said Kenelm. "That'll be the day." But he was off too and running towards Mulberry Lane.

Calli followed with Annie a hair's breadth behind. *Don't eat anything, Minna. Please don't eat anything.*

CHAPTER TWENTY-TWO

Minna's back door was indeed unlocked. Kenelm pulled it open and the cat shot past his ankles. Minna lay on the floor where she'd fallen as she'd tried to stand. A square container of salad sat in the middle of the table. The smell was noticeable.

Instantly, he put out an urgent call on his radio for an ambulance, specifying likely coniine poisoning.

"My feet," whispered Minna. "My legs."

"How much did you eat," said Calli, rushing in with Annie and trying to sit her up.

"Only a taste," came the thread of a voice. "Timmy wanted out."

"He probably saved your life," said Annie. "Keep her warm, Calli. Rub her feet. Keep the circulation going. Don't stop. I need to make you sick, Minna. Sorry."

"Ipecac. Larder," said Minna faintly.

"Good God," said Gideon, arriving with his superfluous toolbox and breathing hard. "Who still has ipecac these days?"

"Minna, evidently," said Calli. "Do you know how to use it?"

"Oh, yes. It was Grandma's favourite answer to bad behaviour." Annie was opening the old-fashioned larder as she spoke, scanning the shelves for the bottle.

"Ambulance is on its way," said Kenelm tersely. "I've given them the details. What I need now is a large bag for the salad tub."

Three hours later they were back in Calli's kitchen and Gideon was ladling the curry on to plates. The shiraz was long gone, but he'd nipped over to the Lodge for a bottle of Merlot.

Kenelm dropped into a chair and drank his first glass straight down, blessing his cousin for the forethought. "I got the station to fingerprint the container as a matter of urgency. Overlapping prints of Heather, Pat, Violet and Minna in that order."

"So we were right," said Calli. "Violet added hemlock to her sister's plate for no other reason than festering hatred and to muddy the water, then brought the leftovers from the talk home, not realising Heather hadn't eaten anything."

He nodded. "We were right, or rather, you were. Irritatingly, so was Macready with his push for accidental death, just not for the reason he thought. I've filed our conjecture regarding the sequence of events. It's up to him if he takes it further."

"And Minna is going to be okay?"

"She should be. They've pumped her stomach, flushed her out and hooked her up to various drips. She'll be home Monday or Tuesday." He looked across to Annie. "I still can't believe you said you'd feed the cat while she was in hospital."

Annie gave an irritable shrug. "I'm not waiting on him hand and foot. Gideon is going to fit a cat flap. Look, someone had to. Worrying won't help her recovery."

Kenelm was beginning to think that underneath Annie's spiky exterior there was an unexpectedly soft centre. "Nor will knowing her best friend was a serial poisoner who was planning to bump her off. Violet had probably been planning it ever since learning Desmond Saxon owned his bungalow and would leave it to his daughter. I wouldn't be surprised if she blackmailed Jerry Ellwood into doing a low valuation on it for probate so Minna wouldn't have to give away any inheritance tax." He grinned at Gideon. "I might ask him, just to give him a hard time. I've also amplified the suggestion to Macready that he looks into deaths-of-best-friends at all her previous addresses. That curry smells epic. Thank you."

"It is epic," said Annie, tearing off a piece of naan to eat with it. "Macready's accidental-death verdict doesn't help Minna."

"Oh, I don't know," said Calli, "she might achieve a strange notoriety. *The Best Friend Who Lived: my escape story."* She glanced at Gideon. "We are going to tell everyone, right?"

Gideon nodded decisively. "We absolutely are. Kenelm's colleagues might never prove it, but it'll scotch the talk here and make life smooth again."

Smooth. Kenelm looked at the pair of them and poured himself another glass of wine. Dee had pinpointed it, Fencross Parva wasn't real life. However, as it appeared to be what he had, he'd live with it. A small measure of familiar fantasy to keep him anchored. He'd deal with reality during working hours.

Sunday afternoon. Annie went into the garden from the studio door and stretched in the spring sunshine. Well-being washed over her for the sheer joy of being able to work for hours undisturbed. She looked back through the door at her easel and at the painting that had been growing all day, a meadow pond, the air rippling with summer heat, tall grass dotted with cornflowers and poppies and meadowsweet. It might not be what Bunty had envisaged, but Annie could *see* it in the rectory sitting room. Large, much larger than this test canvas, vibrant with colour, filling the wall, pulling the outdoors inside.

She walked past the pecking, scratching hens and leant on the fence at the bottom of the garden. Kenelm was on the common, looking relaxed in a rugby shirt and jeans, playing football with his sons. They must keep them fit in the police force. Not many men her age could keep up with a couple of athletic teenagers. She smiled as he tackled his younger son, got the ball, was tackled in turn by the older boy and lost the ball to him. Had he planned that? Some men would, Gideon for example, but Annie didn't think Kenelm was that subtle. He played life straight, to the best of his ability. It was a wonder he'd got as far as he had in the world, except that his best was twice as good again as other people's best.

No one would take him for a policeman today. He looked like any other Fencross Parva dad, comfortable with his boys, as if life could hold no more than this. As if he belonged.

She went back to the studio doorway and looked at her sketch painting again. Her fingers tingled with the rightness of it. Her hand hovered over Bunty's number on her phone.

Sunday evening. Kenelm thumbed his mobile off and put it on the table. For the first time in months he didn't have to stop himself slamming it down. "Amazing. No fault to find apart from the mud on the boys' clothes."

Annie grinned at him from where she was stirring something savoury on the stove. "Good day, then."

"A better day, certainly. I haven't felt as displaced as

usual. I haven't..." *Spit it out, Kenelm.* "I haven't hurt as much. You were right, seeing the boys on neutral ground was good for all of us. Thanks for suggesting it."

"No problem."

Had she realised this was the first time he'd admitted he was hurting? Ah well, in for a penny, in for a pound. "I think what it is... with my marriage breaking down..." He stopped and started again. "I've never failed at anything before."

"Welcome to my world."

And now it was important that she didn't think he was whining. "Come off it, Annie, you're a superwoman with all the balls you juggle. I just want what I've always wanted. To do my job well, to make a difference to society, to come home to companionship. Not to be separated from life like when I was growing up in the Manor. Not to be lonely."

"To belong somewhere?"

He mulled that over. "I suppose so, yes. To belong and to have a small part of the world that was mine. I thought, when I left Fencross Parva the first time and struck out for myself, that I'd found it. I was wrong."

She turned the gas down and put the saucepan lid on. "I wanted to get away too," she said, sitting at the table opposite him. "I wanted to spread my wings and find myself. There was no chance when Grandma was alive. She'd always worked, so she expected everyone else to work. She despised Aunty Dora for going on the stage and finding men to support her. She despised Mum for getting taken in by the first bloke who kissed her and told her she was gorgeous. Mum stuck it out until I went to school, then she got the job at the dry cleaners. And then, despite the fact that she was earning, Grandma despised her even more for chattering and laughing with everyone and going out openly to the cinema and the pub when she ought to have been eaten up with shame for the rest of her days."

"Your mum was a brave woman," commented Kenelm.

"It was her way of taking back a bit of control, of contributing to the household, of saying that she was staying because of me, but on her own terms. She was only twenty-two when I was old enough to go to school, Kenelm. I sometimes have to work very hard not to feel guilty about her giving up the life she should have had for me."

"She wouldn't have done it if she hadn't loved you."

"It took its toll. The more Grandma nagged, the more outrageously she behaved. I didn't even bother fighting my corner when it was my turn. I clung to full-time education until I'd done A-levels, then discovered I had this awkward sense of duty. It surprised the hell out of me. I went to the garden centre at Much Clattering straight from school because at least it was working with plants and it gave me time to draw and save a bit of money and keep the peace at home. I thought I owed it to them both."

"Then that was also brave of you."

She scowled. "It didn't feel brave. I simply couldn't see what else to do. And then… then Grandma died of a heart attack the day after her seventieth birthday, just like that on the street. She left the house to me, actually putting in the will that Mum was too flighty and couldn't be trusted with it and Aunty Dora had chosen her own path years ago."

"So then you felt really guilty?"

"I should have done but I didn't, that came later. I felt liberated like you wouldn't believe. Suddenly I could go to art school. I didn't care that I only went as far as Cambridge and came back here for weekends. I didn't mind being older than the other students and paying my way doing antisocial shifts at the supermarket. I was learning and talking to people who spoke my language and *growing*."

In his mind's eye he saw her again with Heather in the studio. Vital. Glowing. "That must have been wonderful."

She looked at him ruefully. "I knew it was too good to be true. The dry cleaner on Church Parade closed and Mum was transferred to the Newmarket branch where there were more men and more pubs and she got conned by a good-looking bastard gambler ten years younger than her."

"Oscar, yes?"

"That was him. Dancing blue eyes, dark auburn hair, just the hint of an Irish brogue. Charm personified. Fun with a capital F. As soon as I found out what he was really after - from Jerry Ellwood of all people - and informed dear Oscar that the cottage was mine, not Mum's, he left. And so, inch by inch, did Mum's reason."

"You finished your degree?"

"Oh yes, got my qualifications and my skills and my contacts... but the promise of freedom was gone. The lovely, rosy, art-filled life was gone. I had to look after Mum."

"At least you have your own home. You're settled."

He was surprised by the bleakness in her eyes. "Am I? I wasn't away long enough to feel any difference. I don't know whether I'm settled or trapped. Whether I'm contented or hiding from reality. I have no way of knowing, and I will never have any way of knowing because there are care-home fees to be paid, bills to pay, upkeep... You know what houses and families are like, Kenelm. It's endless. I can't stop. I can't just pack my painting satchel and go off on a gap year. I'm tethered."

She was trusting him with her inner feelings. Kenelm felt an astonishing swoop of gratitude. His eyes pricked and he blinked to clear them. "And part of you rages against that and part of you is resigned, because you know you might have chosen it anyway."

She nodded. "It would have been nice to have had the

choice. But I didn't. I couldn't. There was only me. I was the responsible one. I always have been."

Responsible. And that was it, that was the link. An infinitesimal fragment of his heart unfroze. "That's how I've always felt," he said. "With me it was the need to do something worthwhile to atone for my useless, entitled family."

They looked at each other. Unspoken understanding hung in the air.

Kenelm cleared his throat. "I saw Bunty was here before I took the boys home. Is that going okay?"

Annie also took a metaphorical step back. "Yes, she likes the sample sketch. I've got the go-ahead for the big canvas. She might even want more."

"So... if you have Heather's illustration contract as well as Bunty's commission, does that mean you'll give up letting out rooms?"

There was an odd pause. Could it be the idea hadn't occurred to her? "I don't mind you," she said at last. "You're hardly ever here. Be a shame for Gideon to make you a desk and then not use it."

Was that a yes or a no? It was surprisingly important to find out. "Then... may I stay?"

She nodded. "I'd be stupid to turn down regular rent. Besides, with you in that room, making it yours, it keeps Grandma at bay."

"I'll get on to Gideon's electrician first thing tomorrow. I'll even take the dogs out when you're busy working. Thank you."

She lifted her head and smiled at him, a proper smile. It transformed her face and his heart gave the tiniest, tiniest jump. "Busy," she said. "I like the sound of busy."

He smiled back. "Long may it last. I will help, Annie, just tell me what needs doing. I need the stability."

She put out her hand. "Deal."

Relief lightened his mind. He was staggered at how much. A small somewhere to call home. A corner that was his. "Deal," he said, clasping her hand - which was warm and workaday and sensible - for no longer than was conventional.

Because... scars... privacy... trust...

They were friends, and that was very precious right now. One step at a time.

~ ~ THE END ~ ~

ACKNOWLEDGEMENTS

A huge thank you to Louise Allen for encouragement and eagle-eyed scrutiny

Thanks also to Sheila McClure and Lesley Cookman for prodding me to get on with it

Enormous gratitude to Kate Johnson for being there in all those dark nights of the soul when I was unconvinced I could still string words together

Many thanks to Jane Dixon-Smith for another fabulous cover

and thank *you*, if I've forgotten to include you

WORKS BY JAN JONES

<u>Full Length Novels</u>

STAGE BY STAGE – Cambridge set romcom featuring a musical theatre company

A QUESTION OF THYME - herbs, healing and humour: love story with WW1 incursions

DIFFERENT RULES - living, loving and growing in a 1990s Bohemian vicarage

~ Fencross Parva Mysteries~

A BODY IN THE LIBRARY
- contemporary village shenanigans

THE UNPLEASANTNESS AT THE BELLADONNA CLUB - gardening club wars

~ Smoke and Mirrors ~

MYSTERY ON THE PRINCESS LINE - 1920s ocean liner mystery

MYSTERY AT THE BAY SANDS HOTEL - 1920s coastal resort mystery

MYSTERY AT THE BLACK CAT CLUB - 1920s London nightclub mystery

~ Newmarket Regencies ~

THE KYDD INHERITANCE
– secrets and skulduggery in Regency England

FAIR DECEPTION
– secrets and scandal in Regency Newmarket

FORTUNATE WAGER
– secrets and sabotage on the Regency racecourse

AN UNCONVENTIONAL ACT
– secrets and subterfuge in the Regency theatre

~ Furze House Irregulars ~

A RATIONAL PROPOSAL
- cads and card-sharps in Regency England

A RESPECTABLE HOUSE
- scars and scoundrels in Regency Newmarket

A SCHOLARLY APPLICATION
- mysteries and missing persons in Regency Newmarket

A PRACTICAL ARRANGEMENT
- horrors, hopes and happy endings in Regency England

Novellas

THE PENNY PLAIN MYSTERIES

quirky, cosy novellas, set in a harbour town on the edge of the English Lake District

1: THE JIGSAW PUZZLE – old jigsaws, switched paintings, new friendships

2: JUST DESSERTS – ice-cream, jam wars, a lost aeroplane and the WI show

3: LOCAL SECRETS – graffiti, town planning, a local brewery and a WW1 mystery

4: THE CHRISTMAS GIFT – pilfering, old photos and a memorable Nativity

Other novellas

WRITTEN ON THE WIND – trees, old ways & mobiles set on the N.Yorks moors

FAIRLIGHTS – a pele tower overlooking the sea, secrets stretching back for years

WHAT THE EYE DOESN'T SEE – a Flora Swift mystery set in a village post office

AN ORDINARY GIFT – a time-slippish paranormal romantic mystery, set in Ely

ONLY DANCING – a romantic suspense, with 1970s flashbacks

Non Fiction

QL SuperBASIC – the Definitive Handbook

ABOUT THE AUTHOR

Award-winning author Jan Jones was born and brought up in North London, but now lives near Newmarket, equidistant from Cambridge, Bury St Edmunds and Ely. She writes contemporary, mystery, suspense, paranormal and historical romance.

Jan is a vice-president of the Romantic Novelists' Association. Website at https://romanticnovelistsassociation.org/

Jan has won the Elizabeth Goudge Trophy twice (in 2002 and 2019), the RNA Joan Hessayon debut novel award in 2005, and has been shortlisted five times in various RoNA Romantic Novel of the Year categories. She writes books, novellas, serials, poetry and short stories for women's magazines. She can be found at http://jan-jones.blogspot.co.uk/ and is at https://www.facebook.com/jan.jones.7545 for Facebook and on twitter as @janjonesauthor

Fun fact: A former software engineer, Jan co-designed and wrote the Sinclair QL computer language SuperBASIC. Her textbook *'QL SuperBASIC - the Definitive Handbook'* occasionally turns up in second-hand sales, commanding ridiculous sums of money and causing her to wish quite fervently that she'd kept her original author copies. Thirty years later she retyped, reformatted and re-released a Kindle edition of *'QL SuperBASIC - the Definitive Handbook'*. To her astonishment, and with heartfelt gratitude to all those in the QL community, it is still selling steadily.

Printed in Great Britain
by Amazon